Precious
Redemption

Library of Congress Control Number: 2011947675

ISBN: 978-0-9832078-6-3

Printed in the United States of America
Hollywood, Fl

Scripture quotations are taken from the King James Version and the New King James Version of the Bible – except where otherwise noted within.

PECAN TREE PUBLISHING

Hollywood, Fl.
www.pecantreebooks.com

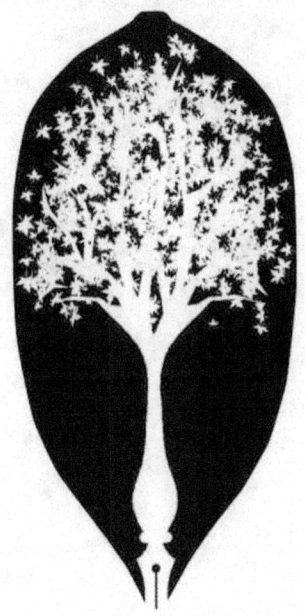

New Voices | New Styles | New Vision

From the Author...

I praise God for what He has done in me, through me, inspire of me. I hope these words and every word I write are pleasing to Him. This Lord is for you.

I praise God for my mother Annie Thomas, my sister Tatiana Lucretia Freeman, my brother Douglas Tirrell Freeman, Sr.; my cousin Annie Bowens, my son Isaiah Langston-Michael Freeman (yes mommy is happy), my nephew Douglas Tirrell Freeman, Jr., my niece Camisha Ann Freeman. I praise God for Deanna Harris, Antinori Harris, Deion McNeil, Tammy Norton and RJ and Tami-jah Scriven. I am grateful to Claudia and Cailin Chastain. I thank you all for being there.

I praise God for Pops, Douglas Charles Freeman— while you have crossed over, I am still very much your girl.

Special thanks to: Paula Belle Wilkes, the Jogging Poet, Tymira Mack, Donna Patton and Out the Box Radio and to each of you.

Precious Redemption

E. Claudette Freeman

I Thessalonians 5:23

"and the very God of peace sanctify you wholly; and I pray God your whole spirit and soul and body be preserved blameless unto the coming of our Lord Jesus Christ."

This is not real

Chapter One

"YAAAAAWWWWW! AAARRRGGGH!"

Hard footsteps. Running. Yelling. Leaves crushing like ice in a blender. Hard and heavy breathing forcing the trees to bend. They seemed to have a rhythm.

"HEL...!"

Something broke. A thud and a breaking. Hard footsteps. Why were their feet hitting the ground so hard? I could hear the thunder before and behind me. I could not see it yet. This wasn't how this day was supposed to be.

"PLEASEEEEE.. GOOO.... GOOO..."

This wasn't how this day was supposed to be. Hell's army was on every side of me. I was in combat mode in my tux, the flower still pinned to my lapel.

I got up early. I never actually went to sleep. If I went to sleep, I told myself, I would oversleep. I would miss a moment that was going to change my life forever. I had gone over all her plans because she forced me to; there was nothing about demonic invasion in the plans.

I got up at 5:30, ran five miles, went to our new home and unpacked the last seven boxes that were delegated to me by the woman whose love electrified me. Then, I went back to my almost empty apartment, stared at the tux and the wedding ring for about an hour, showered and got dressed. I think I arrived at the church before the wedding planner. I sat on the front pew of the church and stayed out of her way. Her razor sharp, mocha-colored face, said, stay out of my way, you groom man who is here too damn early. I stayed in that position until I smelled a soft fragrance. I love that fragrance, and so I turned in the direction of its strongest aroma. There she was. Not in her dress yet, but her hair curled and draping the right side of her face. Of course, it would drape to the right, because I always kiss her on the left. She blew me a kiss and ran off.

When I saw her again, she was in splendor. She seemed to glide through the garden-transformed sanctuary. The moment I inhaled the fullness of my woman, my breaths failed to match my anticipation. My attention to detail was lost in her. I couldn't tell you what the dress looked like. I know initially it was white. She touched it at some point, and glided towards me. Half way down the aisle, the earth shook, the roof came off the church, everything was spinning, and the clouds above all of this colored themselves black. I heard his laugh. That laugh knocked me from the altar and across several pews. She was gone.

"ANTHONYYYYY! HELP – HELP-!"

I shook myself away from these hands. They weren't pulling me up. They were pushing me down. And I could hear her scream. I could hear a voice I didn't know calling me. It never said my name, but I knew it was calling me.

"DAD! DAD! They'll kill us! They'll kill us!"

"ANTTTT. COME ...."

She was gone. Every face in this realm laughed at me. Where did she go? And who was calling me? I fought my way through the front doors of the church. Fighting through the worse smells I've ever encountered. Stench choked me; invaded my nostrils, my lungs. Fighting with forces grabbing at me, claws slicing through my tuxedo. My foot planted solid against the doors knocked them off the hinges. I followed the doors, falling head first into dark woods. It was wet and cold.

"ANTTTTT. COME...."

To my right I saw her. Her splendor soiled by their hand prints, mud trails like draped jewels across her beauty. I took off towards her and about 10 lunges in, these arms locked around me and tossed me in the opposite direction. My body crashed against a tree and I slid into the mud.

"YAAAAAWWWWW! AAARRRGGGH!"

Hard footsteps. Running. Yelling. Leaves crushing like ice in a blender. Hard and heavy breathing forcing the trees to bend. They seemed to have a rhythm.

"HEL...!"

This wasn't how this day was supposed to be! I heard their voices in unison, cut through my very spirit.

"DADDY!"

"ANTHONY!"

"KILL THEM!"

Then nothing. I took another step and was jolted when I felt myself falling. The motion of it shook me awake. I grabbed the side of the mattress – I guess – to keep from hitting the ground. There she was; sound asleep, her night tank top ruffled just above her waist. I slid to my side of the bed, facing our wedding portrait and stared it for a moment. The urgency of her voice in the dream pulled me to the painting, and I stood their stroking it. Suddenly, without any sane reason in mind, I ran to her side of the bed and assured – well, kissed her lightly on the neck, then climbed into bed and pulled her into my arms.

We were married three nights before that nightmare. Why it invaded my thoughts, as I held her slumbering frame in my arms, made beads of sweat dance across my scalp. And, still, the voices cut through my very spirit.

"KILL THEM!"

Finally, in love

Chapter Two

I stood at the door of the bedroom taking in the coolness of the room. For whatever reason, it seemed that the normal 72 setting on the central air conditioner felt colder, like winter chill in the air. I suddenly noticed that the feng-shui of the room was exceptional. Remodeled to make me comfortable and relaxed in every corner; I smiled as I saw the gazebo peeping through the blinds. When they were pulled back the picture window revealed a line of orange and mango trees, and a flower garden that lifted sweet fragrances at various times of the year. These were trees I'm sure with history. Grand limbs touched as if they were beckoning each other to dance. The fruit, when born in their season, was always plump and sweet. Though I do not like mangoes, I've discovered that they are a wonderful aphrodisiac to a man that does enjoy their taste. The oranges, I thought as I enjoyed the site of the blossoms, would be in soon and I would get a kick out of squeezing them for breakfast or sitting in the gazebo and eating them. There have been times since we've moved into this hidden area of Miami Lakes, or the

Country Club of Miami, depending on who you ask with its mini-palaces and delicate mix of old school Anglo and Hispanic money, progressive Black money, and a comical mix of bourgeois, gothic and hip hop wanna-be teenagers; that I've literally eaten four or five oranges back to back sitting in that gazebo.

My girl Maggie mocks my wonderful gazebo often, "you couldn't get your average white plastic kind of gazebo - no - yours would have to look exotic like something out of Caribbean or African travel magazines. What is this - tooth picks on steroids?" It did look that way, but the gazebo, which was wonderfully crafted with bamboo poles, had to compliment the flow of the trees. Surely, I thought, the essence of blossoms, and red and orange fruit would be lost as art playing above and around a simple white structure. They all had a purpose. That purpose - simply celebrate the fact that you are part of a tremendous painted canvas that God himself constantly re-creates.

The view to garden and gazebo, in fact the garden and gazebo themselves, are my come to Jesus place. The place where I sit - often without saying a word - and bear my soul to The Wonder. This is the no pretense place. When I am in this place, I give no care to what else is happening in the seven bedrooms, the living room that I still think is way too big, the kitchen that my husband says belongs in a house with a cook staff, nor the four bathrooms. One of my bathrooms doesn't really know it's a bathroom - it's more like a sink room. This sink room is where I've begun to hide the stuff I buy that I need to sneak into the house gradually.

This bedroom, however, is our sanctuary. We had agreed that this one room in the house would represent tranquility and so we decorated it with blues and greens. Very soft fabrics sashay across the windows. There are oversized pillows and two love seats with huge cushions that embrace you like winter comforters when you sit down. A king size bed which is way too big considering the way we slept. Honestly, it could have easily been a twin bed and there would still be room left over. As I enjoyed those very colors at this moment, the room seemed to beckon me to a place where my mind could chill and my heart could feel open to the love in this room.

My mind did need to chill. Lately, between horrific nightmares and periods of intense self-interrogation I was beginning to experience headaches like never before. While he has not said anything, something troubling Anthony's sleep – again – has also troubled mine. In this moment, however, my mind was filled simply with the pleasure of this place.

I watched my husband peaceful in his slumber and praised God that I could see his steady breaths in the movement of his chest. His face was comfortable even in this state of sedation. There was something about him at this moment that wanted me to wake him up and cuddle him. I've seen women do that to newborn babies. I imagine that they, like I, want to simply love on that humble-ness, that innocence, that joy that drapes them in their sleep. His chest gently rose and fell in a steady matter and I knew that he was all right. Not that he had been sick or anything; I was just thankful that I have a man, a husband, someone that has loved me despite my out of control inquisitiveness and my ability to do everything he tells me not to.

Honestly, I don't think I purposely do everything he tells me not to – I just understand that Ant and I see things differently. I understand that he does not see the need for me to buy two of the same dresses in different sizes. But, there are certain days of each month that I am going to be a tad bit bloated, so the size 10 I normally wear would fit like a size 8 on me; while the second dress, which I bought as a 12 will fit like the size 10 that I really am. Anthony says that's crazy and vain since no one really knows for five days out of the month, I'm wearing a size 12 that looks like a size 10. I say women know and the 12 will hide the puffiness that the 10 won't. So, part of what's in the bathroom (that doesn't know it's a bathroom) is a whole bunch of size 12 dresses and size 14 jeans. Marriage has done wonders for my hips.

I also am fully aware that I can write, from a strictly qualified to do so perspective, articles on health and little flowery feature items, as opposed to my usual cutting edge crime, social dysfunction kind of pieces. Those are no fun and I get bored with them so quickly that it takes me three days to write one 750 words article. I cannot do those and he cannot understand it. For a time, after we first got married, I tried. I did several pieces on breast cancer, which I liked. I did some book and movie reviews. Even did a column for a while on life management principles from a Christian perspective. I honestly got a kick out of each of them. Yet, every time I sat down to write during what I now call my "housewife writing period," all I heard in my head was - blah blah, nothing juicy, blah blah blah, is anything major gonna happen here, blah blah blah blah, okay well can we just go to sleep now. It just was not me. I must have something that is going to make me think, reason, look beyond and over every possible scenario. Anything that is going to thrill my mind, challenge my preconceptions, catch me off guard is what I'm getting into. What's funny about that to me is, while those are the things about me that drives Ant so crazy, those are the very same things that attracted me to him. He caught me off guard, gliding into my path when I had sworn off men. Challenging my preconceptions about men in Christ and to this day, he thrills so much more than just my mind.

After having my heart handed back to me time and time again or passed around like a bottle of gin in a brown paper bag beneath the liquor store tree – I admit, hindsight made me wiser. I mean think about it, any man that can't pick up a phone to call at least twice a week is not interested in a serious relationship. Any relationship that mandates you spend time together two counties away from where you live, may mean there is a problem. Any time you can't go to a man's house to spend time with him, you may need to question whether he's still living with his mama, his wife, or someone else. I had come to a point where I could not blame any of the men I had been involved with. The decision to get involved or stay involved was ultimately mine. It wasn't about any of them. It was about me.

I had determined that there had to be at least two things that I appreciated about each guy I had loved. I focused on those two positive things and decided

because there was something good, then the relation-
ships were good. And they each had shaped me into
a better, wiser and higher esteemed woman. Maggie
thought the process was futile. "They were jerks, call them
jerks, and move on." Not. You see I believe when you end
with anger, bitterness and resentment you hold on to that
relationship until you let that stuff go. Yet, if you can find
the two good things, you instead celebrate the possibilities and in the process, assemble a list of what really gets
you and keeps you with a man. Especially if you don't
include sex as one of the two things.

Like I said, hindsight made me wiser. Thanks, be to
God; He is still in the prayer answering business. Boy had
I been praying, not for a man, but for my former men and
for myself. I had to forgive me, and them, and I had to
pray that there was nothing that we would hold against
each other that was against God's purpose for each of us.
Then I prayed that He would simply prepare me for what
His will was for me. That I would begin to love and be
with Him the way I had been with my various lovers. He
answers prayers. Because He does, I am glad and hon-
ored that I had finally been blessed. I appreciate the fact
that I still feel like I have "finally" been blessed – although
Anthony and I have been together in marriage almost five
years. It is refreshing that I can still look at this man and
think "finally."

People probably never really think about how awesome it is months, years into a marriage to look at the
person you made this major commitment with and feel
like you just fell in love. The first year of our marriage, I
spent a lot of time being constantly frantic. I could not

believe I deserved someone that would look in my eyes, and tell me that *"unconditional is just the beginning of how much I love you."* Hearing those words made everything in my spirit tremble and for the first time in a long time, my heart felt like it didn't need to hold on to the old Band-Aids just in case.

I know, does that mean the two good things philosophy doesn't work? No, it just means that sometimes letting go of the good things still cut. So even in hearing him say those words, there was this nagging no-good voice in the back of my head that kept saying 'you know this is not going to last', 'anything that good can't really be good for you', 'just wait his true colors would show'. Why was that? I mean really, why do people think that way. If you pray to be blessed with this awesome husband and then you are blessed with him, then why doubt it? A lot of those naysayers are no longer close to me. I mean why keep people around who are pessimistic and opinionated about your good thing when their thing isn't even a thing and if it is a thing, it's a thing they're not spending enough time on because they're too focused on your thing. Nevertheless, as I glanced at him in peaceful slumber, I smiled. Smiled at the joy of my man thing, my love thing, my life thing – arousing my fancy.

Lord, can I have him?

Chapter Three

I met Anthony Houston, amazingly not at the church we both attended, but at a Vickie Winans concert. Vickie, an amazing gospel artist with ridiculous vocal range, was right in the midst of one her comedic sketches before she gets to the next song, when I heard him apologize for having to step across me. I tried to ignore the fact that this brother was smelling good and was wearing the hell out of that green linen suit. I mean wearing it to the point that it looked like every quarter inch of fabric was tailored to fall perfectly on the piece of body that it covered. What a piece of body it was too. Not that I hadn't seen good looking brothers before, but this boy just ... took my whole attention for an amazing few seconds. I liked the sound of his voice when he called me Miss. It wasn't one of those heavy baritone voices, nor was it a soft and smooth kind of voice either. It was, I don't know, a classic kind of deep male voice. That voice said, 'yeah you can call me late at night and say my name over and over again.' That voice was very humble, warm, smooth, and confident. For about thirty good seconds I don't know what Vickie was singing or saying.

While a gospel concert was probably not the place to start lusting, I must admit that I was completely taken aback by this tall drink of water in a major relationship drought in my life. And a drought following days caught up in countless relationship Ferris wheels, was not very much fun. The carnival rides and the drought had made me very cautious when it came to choosing my own interest and very not wanting to get involved with anyone while I got deeper involved with me and God. That however did not stop me from watching him throughout the show, nor did it stop the desire to hold him when I saw him crying as Vickie sang, *"oh what love He has for me, that He would give his life."*

Watching him deal with whatever moment he was having with God, I found myself shaking my head. Not because I thought 'what a wimp!' But because I thought, my God – that's beautiful. How awesome it is to see a Black man so into you that in a room full of thousands of people, he doesn't mind submitting to you enough to cry in public. What a beautiful thing. Typically, the Black man, or men in general, are not ones for outward displays of emotion. Men are certainly not creatures that tear up in public, except for maybe a funeral here or there. Yet, here stood this giant, arms extending towards heaven in submission, tears streaming not trickling, streaming down his face. Here, not even a good four feet from me, stood this beautiful brown angel, his body heaving as he released every bit of his soul. I felt myself entangled in his pain at that moment and it nearly spilled over into my own tears, until I redirected my attention to the song and quietly asked God to hold him in his sorrow. Okay, then I had to repent, because the next thought was, "Lord, can I have him?"

By the end of the concert I was tired, between the three choirs that sang before Vickie and her making you cry with laughter and then cry in praise – I was literally exhausted. I thought about the nights I had spent rotating from club to club just a few years ago, and could not remember clubbing to the point that I was this tired. That was cool, number one considering most of my clubbing nights I was supposed to be in church and number two, I know that what tired me out tonight was the power and glory in the house. I walked away from the church tired but spiritually and emotionally invigorated. I gathered my purse from the seat next to me and adjusted my dress as I stood. I glanced back at the green linen suit to see if maybe I could or should offer him something. A tissue, some kind words, something. When I did look back, he had composed himself and was heading out the opposite side of the pew.

I walked the two blocks back to my car only to discover that I had a very definite flat tire. A very definite flat tire on my brand-new truck - that I was not in the mood to change. I fumbled through my purse, which was way too full of a bunch of stuff I really did not need for a gospel concert, in search of my cell phone to call road service and to find someone to pick me up. At 11:45 at night in an area close to Liberty City, one of Miami's oldest Black neighborhoods and painted with strokes of rampant violence and drugs, according to the media, road side assistance would not put me on their priority list, so someone to pick me up was a good move. I laughed thinking about how so many people would avoid this part of town, yet like any other community it had generations of families that still lived here, it had birthday celebrations, graduation parties, and weddings full of love. Yet you never saw those things flashing across the screen even on a horribly slow news day. No, you only heard about the drug bust in the housing developments or the street gang that operated out of a corner store.

As I pondered how I might be able to turn that into a story, I realized my keys were slipping from my hands quickly. But, in an effort not to drop my keys, I ended up dropping the cell phone, which displayed its gymnastics ability by doing a nicely formatted bounce from the side rail and a nicely executed flip beneath the truck. So here was my dilemma, do I walk two blocks back to the church for help or do I hike up my kicking Donna Karan dress and climb under the truck to get the phone. Staring at the ground in a total state of "what is this, what is this" I was waving my free hand in the air like a mad woman. That's when I heard that newly familiar voice behind me.

"If you move over a little bit, I'll get that for you."

I tried to pretend like my heart rate had not just increased fourfold when I turned around to see that the tall, green linen suit looked even better up close. Baby boy was a nice pecan color, with these incredible deep dimples, warm brown eyes and these full well-formed lips. Standing before me, I realized he easily was six foot three and the reason the suit hung on him the way it did was because there was all over firmness. The suit had no choice but to hang just so. It hung like a woman afraid to let go of her man in public. Truly not wanting to be embarrassed by the fact that I was lovingly watching his lips, I began to speak.

"Thank you, I would appreciate it. I was trying not to drop the keys, and ended up dropping the phone. Wait a minute. Let me see if I've got something in the truck to put down there so you don't get your pants dirty."

"Don't sweat it. Clothes go to the cleaners. I pay them to get out whatever I get in." He had a very shy smile and obviously, a quick wit. I liked that. I liked the way he could extend his body in a push up form and reach beneath the truck with ease.

"That would be true." I suddenly thought about what I must look like to him. There was a nice breeze blowing and I certainly hoped that my hair was not all over the place and what he saw was a peacock with fully displayed feathers. I hadn't freshened up my lipstick. I didn't know if my dress was accentuating all the proper assets. Why is it you can never do your inventory before the brothers you want to notice you - notice you?

That was the one night that I took extra effort and joy making sure Maggie felt bad about missing. Between her job and me meeting deadlines on three projects, one of which was a serious investigative piece on community development corporations misusing grant monies and not providing promised services, Mags and I had not seen each other. That was unusual for us. We kind of kept each other going through the challenging days and the lonely nights. We covered each other spiritually, financially and I guess like girls do in every regard. I kind of missed her, even though at the time we only lived maybe five miles from each other. Life and its movements can make five miles seem like five thousand. We were going to catch up that night. We would probably have left the concert and went to my place - made a big pot of sausage stew and yellow rice and ate it all laughing and comparing notes on what we had and had not done. Then we'd talk about where each pound of sausage was going to settle on our bodies. She would probably assess that the kiel-basa would show up in her upper arms, while the Italian sausage would add three more inches on her butt. Weight always settled in my thighs and along my waist - so I con-stantly worked out. I worked out because I love to eat and I was never the kind of person that figured I should not eat anything I enjoyed – because of calories or fat grams or any other gram.

We had purchased these tickets three weeks ago, made a whole night's itinerary and then three hours before the show and our night on the town, she decides to go to work. Oh, I could not wait to call that good sister up and vividly and slowly start describing this brother, only to suddenly drop the call. Which is what I did; followed by not answering when she called back three times in a row. I remember thinking, "I got a fine piece of man under my truck playing knight in shining armor and if I had not gotten saved, I would take him home tonight." Honestly, up until about a year ago, saved and all, I would probably have at least asked him to go home with me.

"I said, do you have a spare? Miss!"

"A spare what sugar? I mean a spare what?"

"Tire. You do know your tire is flat?"

His raised eyebrows seemed to indicate he was getting a kick out of my distraction. He noticed what I thought I was being very discreet about.

"I'm sorry, my mind drifted off. Yes, I have one. I can't ask you to do that. I can call road service; someone will pick me up."

"I can change it. I wouldn't feel right leaving you out here like this. Why don't you get in your truck and lock the door; I'll go bring my car up here."

I didn't even protest. Something was in the works and who am I to mess with God's plan; especially if it meant I could get to know him. I watched him do a steady run about a block from where I sat. What a sight! A six foot three brother with slightly bowed legs in a well-paced sprint, have mercy! I have a thing for tall brothers. I have a thing for bald brothers. Here's the thing my attraction to men is weird. I can't really tell you what my flavor is - because it varies. I like tall skinny brothers who are deep and radical. I like thick, bald brothers with that 'I'll snatch you' attitude. I like tall, good looking, thick men with broad smiles and general sex appeal. I like a brother that can expound on the Bible and leave you totally amazed in his knowledge. Now, if it's possible to get all of that rolled up into one, that would be - well - THE MAN. But what had fallen into my path after the concert seemed at least on the surface to be close. The smile, the height, the sex appeal, the male confidence, some kind of relationship with God – he was working the details on my list of desires.

As he pulled his car around so that his headlights faced the flat tire, he motioned for me.

"Sit in my car while I do this. By the way - Anthony Houston." I was so caught up in the fact that he had a name I didn't even see him extend his hand. When I realized it, I reached back hoping there was no sweat or nothing that was going to embarrass me.

"I'm sorry." His hands were warm and big. He seemed to swallow my hand in his, his grip pressing my ring into my skin.

"My name is Anthony Houston. Don't I know you from somewhere? We've seen each other before, right?" He released his grip and stepped back as though looking at my whole body would bring something to his remembrance. All I hoped was that he was enjoying the view. Still, I did not know this man so the best thing to do was probably going to be to play it smart and keep my defense up.

"Mr. Houston, don't knights in shining armor have better lines than that?"

"If I was looking for a line, I'd just say let me take you to get something to eat after I change this tire. You go to Triumph Baptist Church, don't you?

"Yes, I do. I'm usually there for the early service and/ or the night service." Is it possible that this brother had noticed me, but I had not noticed him? Honestly, it was possible, no it was probable. I had been through so much drama and so many church-boy players that when I was in church, I kept my focus on God and the Word being taught. I did not stop for conversations. I did not stop for introductions. I know that I had been labeled a snob and probably even worse. It didn't matter, after all this was my time, my heart, my body and I choose what to do with them all.

I also knew that I had probably been labeled a first lady hopeful, to some degree, at Triumph. While every woman I'm sure wants to be involved with a man of power and prestige, I did not think a relationship with my pastor was a good thing. I was wined and dined discreetly and very impressively for weeks under the guise of possibly doing a biography. Yet when the offer was to close the deal with a night in his arms and not a check, I had begged his pardon and let him know that would not be happening. Maggie said she thought that I should leave Triumph after that. How can you sit under a man that tried to get your stuff? - she would ask. Because he did not get it, I told her; and his teaching is solid.

"Then that's where I've seen you. You're usually with a young lady - right?"

"She had to work tonight. But we had the tickets, so I figured one of us should enjoy the show. I know I'm a little scattered right now with the flat tire and all, but did you just ask me out – I mean to get something to eat?"

"No. Not at all. I just let you know I've been watching you - and - I want to take you to get something to eat. You would think a lady in distress would listen for a line a little better."

"Okay. You got me there."

He unbuttoned his shirt and pulled it away from his body and all I could do was hope he didn't hear the gasp of breath I released in that moment of awe. Number one - I was in total shock that this man just took his shirt off in front of a stranger as if it was no big deal. Number two - I was in total shock that what was revealed beneath the shirt was a lovely six pack that did not need to be displayed in front of a lonely heart like me; especially one experiencing that high level of sexual tension right before that time of month. And here is a six pack beneath a chest that I promise you had a reach out and touch me sign hanging across it. Number three - I was thrown off by the fact that he didn't even seem to be concerned with whether or not I was checking him out. Was he just that arrogant? Or was it just taking off a shirt to change a tire?

"Will you lay that across the passenger seat for me please?" I laid the shirt across the leather seat and did a quick once over to see if there were any signs of family. No female slippers lurking around, no lipstick in the cup holder and no car seat or little toys. Good taste in music. Clean and tidy. No cigarette, cigar or reefer residue.

"What is that you've got playing in the car?"

"Kirk Whalum. The Gospel According to Jazz Two. You like that?"

"It's calming."

I rested my head on his seat as he set about changing the tire. Allowing the calming sound of the CD to fill me, I closed my eyes to take in the moment. I heard Mr. Anthony Houston singing with who I was sure was Jonathan Butler accompanying Kirk Whalum, *"falling in love with Jesus, falling in love with Jesus, falling in love with Jesus was the best thing I've ever done. In His arms, I feel protected. In His arms, I'm never disconnected. In His arms, I feel protected – there's no place I'd rather be. There's no place I'd rather be."*

He stopped singing when the instrumental praise rose and Butler ad-libbed the praise. There it was again, though I really was not trying to keep a tally, he had just picked up another impress point. Nice singing voice and not ashamed to sing Jesus as opposed to R. Kelly in the presence of a woman.

"Do you want to eat? Or should I just follow you somewhere? And no, I'm not trying to find out where you live."

"Okay – don't knock a girl for being cautious. I'd like to get a bite to eat. I have to warn you though; I have a healthy appetite."

"Will you do me a favor?"

"Pay for dinner? Just how much does changing a tire go for these days?"

"I don't know. How much does a private investigator go for these days?"

"I'm sorry."

"I saw you checking out the car. I'm not married. I have no kids. I have an aunt and a cousin that I spend time with. And yes, I do work out regularly."

"How very arrogant of you Mr. Houston."

"Arrogant of me - wow - you get snappy when you're hungry huh - healthy appetite?"

"Healthy...oh, okay smart guy - it's Crystal. Crystal Adams. What did you want me to do for you?"

"I want to change into a pair of jeans in my trunk. I'll stand between the doors if you cover the middle."

I watched him pull a pair of jeans and a t-shirt from his trunk after he wiped his hands on a towel. He approached the two open doors and positioned himself between them. Once again, I was thrown off; he was truly just too comfortable with me.

"Okay, Ms. Adams, the shirt was one thing. But I'm not dropping my pants in front of you."

"What?" He circled the air with his finger and I blushed realizing I was facing this man with no shirt on and his belt and pants buttons standing open. "There's that arrogance again. Does it always just pop out like that."

"I have a feeling it pops out about as much as yours does. By the way, I like that fragrance you're wearing."

I turned around and caught this awfully interesting smile curling up on his face. While I wasn't sure what the smile on his face meant; I had a feeling it had something to do with the way the 'fragrance' I was wearing looked from behind. Didn't matter though because hearing the compliment felt good. I had been blessed to, at least, in the very least, have met a new friend on that night.

There were nights in the beginning that Anthony would wake up drenched in sweat and he would have this look of utter terror in his eyes. But he would never talk about it. He'd just look at me and beg me to hold on to him.

"No matter what sugar – I need you to never let me go – will you do that? Will you never let me go girl?"

"I won't let go baby. I promise you Anthony. You are mine."

"No matter what, Crystal? No matter what."

"No matter boo. I'll always hold you just like this."

I would speculate about what would trouble a man so much that sleep was not an option. What kinds of demons were chasing him? I remember hearing old folks say that kids who would toss wildly in their sleep were being ridden by the devil. He would toss for a while, wake up drenched and beg me not to let him go. I started keeping a small towel next to the bed, that I would use to blot the sweat from his face, his head, his chest. Then quietly, as I would hold his warm head against my breast and stroke his smooth oily bald head, he would pray. He would pray, and cry and then pray some more until God gave him peace. Then he would tighten his grip around my waist and fall soundly asleep.

After a while the things that would force him to wake up in his sleep must have dissipated. When I would press him about it, he would tell me that he was not the subject of one of my articles and besides, "when I wake up, I don't remember anything, except feeling this real lightness. Like waking up was some kind of deliverance." I couldn't begin to fathom what happened in those dreams. After about a year of so the nightmares were gone. But Anthony's desire to lay his head on my breast and pray never did leave. I love the fact that it didn't. When I asked him one day not too long ago why still he does that; he smiled, that same sly smile I remember from the first night I met him. "Something about hearing your heart beat and listening to the Lord at the same time lets me know that I finally understand that love is a real thing." My little ego got all pumped up then and all I could say was, "Well, awright boo – I can feel that too." Then he made love to me in the green room, our guest room, and asked if there was a reason we had not yet consummated our marriage in every room in the house.

Just as I prepared to burst out laughing from the memory of our horseplay immediately following that conversation, Anthony began to stir. Whoo, that man knows he can wear a pair of boxers. You know I am truly thankful that if you just believe and trust in His will, God will give you the desires of your heart. And looking at Anthony now I can attest that while I received the desires of my heart, I have also been doused in that exceedingly, abundantly more than you can think or ask blessing thing. I saw a smile brighten his face as he struggled to open his eyes without allowing the rising sun to become uncomfortable.

Kneeling next to him and kissing him softly on his cheeks I thought about what was happening in our lives now that would cause the sweat episodes to return and why they would trouble me deep in the night. We were happy. We'd started talking about having a family. We'd paid off the house and were planning to take a trip to Africa, simply because it was somewhere I had always wanted to visit. Anthony was traveling a lot, but that was not unusual. In fact, we started doing little stupid things just to find different ways to say hurry home. Like he left home on a Tuesday headed to Houston and arrived at the hotel to find a pair of tie up lace panties in his shaving bag. When he got to Los Angeles on Thursday, he mailed me a pair of his boxers. When he arrived home on Saturday, the big raggedy Ann doll he won for me at the Youth Fair met him at the door wearing the rest of that Victoria's Secret outfit that greeted him out west earlier that week.

The only thing that seemed a little out of place was that Anthony had begun talking about his mother a lot. He had never done that. All that I knew was that she died during childbirth and he has never mentioned a father. But with all our conversations about having kids, I understood that part of him wanting to be a father must have ignited his desire to be a son too. Beyond his mother and an Aunt and cousin Nisa that I had met, Anthony didn't discuss family. If the aunt was ever married, I didn't know about it. He was something crazy for Nisa though, at times when we would all spend time together, he holds on to her like their lives depended on each other. I thought to myself one day that if she were not related to him, I would be jealous - that's how strong his love for her is.

She looks like Anthony too. He spoils her to no end and tells me once ours his born - there will be no stopping him. "Spoiling a child", I chided him one day, "makes them lazy and too dependent." He kissed him lightly on my neck and asked and "spoiling a woman makes her what?" Reminding me at that moment of his continual and daily spoiling of me was, in my opinion, unnecessary roughness on the play. I could see very clearly in his relationship with Nisa that he would be a good father. Where he would learn what he needed to know in that role was unclear. Since he didn't mention a father, and neither did Nisa - hers or Ant's, I assumed that the father figures were absent and uncounted for and not worthy of discussion. Still, the more he talked about his mom, the more I watched him with Nisa - the more I knew I'd better quickly get rid of the birth control pills hid in the bathroom that doesn't know it's a bathroom.

I also started to wonder if the nightmares that I was now experiencing were the same things Anthony saw. I mean I have never been one to have nightmares. I could remember maybe one and it was after seeing The Amityville Horror on TV when I was kid. I remember Ant saying before that he had not been one to be plagued with

31

nightmares either and he assumed it was one of the new
life side effects. So maybe the idea of becoming a mother,
going to Africa and maybe moving to Los Angeles where
Ant was spending a lot of time meant the new life side
effects were now on me. I could see these night images
so vividly. The reels of the real-life movie would play
viciously through my mind. It's like they were urging me
to get involved in the madness they portrayed. Over and
over the scenes of pain tossed in my head, the anguish of
these dreams or thoughts or nightmares would cause me
to toss and turn and turn and toss and fight in bed.

Vividly, painfully, urgently these things kept playing
in my head. There was the pretty little angel, dressed in
her satin and lace pink dress, her little hands clapping as
the white gloves kept them warmed, yet her face ... her
face was all grown up and tears rushed from her eyes, and
the hem of the satin and lace dress was soiled. Even in my
sleep, my spirit would let me know that the pretty little
dress was soiled with unmentionable fluid and blood. I
would try to reach her to grab her away. Something was
hurting her and I wanted to rescue her, but every time I
thought I had hold of her, the scene would change or she
would run away. Then I would wake up in tears feeling as
though the fruit of my womb was being defiled. I could
not understand why.

There was the tall and lanky brother, who would keep
whirling and whirling and whirling, his arms tucked
about his body as though he was hiding his very life in his
bosom. As he whirled, I could plainly see blood painting
the walls around him and splattering on the very polished
and shiny black patent leather loafers of men, or maybe

it was just one man? I couldn't really see how many, but I remembered these shoes because they kept showing up in these nightmares. Anyway, this tall, lanky brother in the scene, he's whirling and the blood painted the walls around him and then he would begin to gasp for air and to grasp for something. Was it the blood pouring from his body? Was it the life being beaten from him? Was it the safety of the man in the very polished and shiny black patent leather loafers? And because he grabbed at something, I would grab at something and did not know what. But, just like the little one with the grown-up face, I kept trying to reach him, to grab him, to pull him away – but he would just twirl back into the beatings and I would wake up grabbing at something and hearing him yell.

There was a scene where there was another precious, brown little girl huddled in the back seat of a station wagon, her little body folded like a nice, crisp business shirt. These big huge brown, almost beige eyes would be staring right at me. Next to her, folded just as neatly was a little boy just a little older than she was that would say to her every time the dreams happened, 'ssh.... They're just fussing; they're just fussing.' Sometimes I would feel my breathing getting heavier and heavier as I waited for the next scene. The fussing would creep slowly, getting louder and louder and louder until it was just outside the back seat of the car. Then suddenly like a racquet meets the skin of a tennis ball, he, I guess the husband - would slam her, I guess the wife - against the car and the four little eyes would freeze open for the longest time, never blinking, just frozen on the scene, watching as the blood poured from her eyes and her body would slide down the frame of the car. Then baby girl with the brown eyes would look back at me and shake her head slowly and start to cry.

Shaking her head slowly, crying – her lifeless stare telling me she knew there was no way out of this for her. She would see me the next time I stepped into this evil theater. She would see the woman's face slammed against the window and she would see her pained tears streaking through the streams of blood. Then I would wake up screaming "deliver me, deliver me … oh My God where is the deliverance? You promised me Lord, you promised me. "

Letting all of this and the questions of why, what and where could all of this possibly be coming from take hold of me; I laid my head on Anthony's chest and began to cry. He rose and pulled me to him, lightly kissing my tears away and assured me this would be all right. So, I kissed him and thanked him for his protection. He never questioned me about what I saw. Yet, he would look deep into my eyes whenever he re-assured me, as though he was not speaking to me but to the source of the nightmares. There was something eerie yet comforting about those moments. This time when he looked through me, he said something that made me feel like I needed to hold what he was saying in my bosom. "Crys, there is nothing in anything you see that can hurt you unless you let it."

We parted quietly that morning. He had slept rather late so I knew he was tired, after all another night of my tossing and turning could not have made slumber an easy task. And I'm sure the fact that I had tried to make him remember what his nightmares were about the night before bothered him as well. Whatever he did remember, he did not want to and more importantly, he did not want me trying to drag it out of him for psychoanalyzing.

I however, was determined I was going to figure out what this foolishness in my head was about. I sat quietly in what I thought had to be the biggest black recliner Lazy Boy had ever made. This chair went with nothing in our house. But it was the one piece of furniture Anthony refused to get rid of from his old apartment. His 'something in this house is going to be all about me' stand. I really didn't fight with him but he had a twenty-minute dissertation prepared and it all came flying out when I asked one question, "where are we going to put this?" Oh boy, not only did I realize that I must have already developed a habit of questioning him, but he and that chair had also developed a very personal relationship. There really was no need for the dissertation, after all, he had given up every piece of furniture, except the chair and made sure whatever we purchased in our new house was cool with me. Now I sit in this chair more than he does.

I thought about all that had flooded my mind that morning. Why did I remember that first year of my marriage? Why did I remember Anthony and those cold sweat episodes? Why did the black loafers in the nightmares stick out? Was I doing what I normally do - making one humongous mountain out of what really was just a teeny-weeny mole hill? Why was I interrogating myself? Consumed by the basic questions every journalist learns in news writing 101 – I let go of the crescendo of possibilities begging for my exploration and cast my cares on God.

In the stillness of my humming a praise song I could still hear my great-grandmother sing so clearly – a passage of scripture came ringing clear to my mind and so I said the words as they fell one by one into my spirit.

I waited patiently for the Lord and He inclined to me, and heard my cry. He also brought me up out of a horrible pit, out of the miry clay and set my feet upon a rock and established my steps. He has put a new song in my mouth – praise to our God; many will see it and fear, and will trust in the Lord. Blessed is that man who makes the Lord his trust, and does not respect the proud, nor such as turn aside to lies.

Many, O Lord my God are your wonderful works which you have done; and your thoughts toward us cannot be recounted to you in order; if I would declare and speak of them, they are more than can be numbered. Sacrifice and offering you did not desire; my ears you have opened. Burnt offering and sin offering you did not require. Then I said, "Behold, I come' in the scroll of the book it is written of me. I delight to do your will, o my God, and your law is within my heart.

I have proclaimed the good news of righteousness in the great assembly; indeed, I do not restrain my lips, of Lord, you yourself know. I have not hidden your righteousness within my heart; I have declared your faithfulness and your salvation; I have not concealed your loving-kindness and your truth from the great assembly. Do not withhold your tender mercies from me, o Lord; let your loving-kindness and your truth continually preserve me. For innumerable evils have surrounded me..."

I moved the Bible away from my breasts and began to search for the book where these words came from. It was not a passage that I recognized as something I stored in memory so I knew it was the voice of the Lord offering counsel. His will was for something to be declared before the assembly and based on the dreams it was not to be an easy task. And as I saw the words tucked neatly in Psalm 40; I heard my great grandmother encouraging Miss Jean after she lost her husband, her house, her car and her daughter in a three-month period; "don't let yourself believe the devil got the victory. What you loss you gone surely get back double, if you hold on to the right hand of God. Job lost everything and had to listen to his old complaining friends and a nagging woman through all his pain. But looka here, didn't the Lord give it all back to him and then some?"

As I prepared to close the Word, and rise to face the day – I had to heed one more still voice and that was the one that led me to Jeremiah ten and verse eleven.

"Thus you shall say to them: "the gods that have not made the heavens and the earth shall perish from the earth and from under these heavens."

This verse was just as strong in the New Living Translation:

"Say this to those who worship other gods: "Your so-called gods, who did not make the heavens and earth, will vanish from the earth."

Feeling an overwhelming rush of emotions rising from the bottom of my feet and rushing through my whole being, I fell to my knees. Still overcome, I had no option but to give in to whatever was taking me over and

I lay prostrate. With nothing - but everything - clamoring in my mind, I did what I've heard preacher after preacher say, "when you can't do nothing else, call on the Lord." And I did. When I rose that evening, in bed, I realized Anthony must have put me there. Once again, the dreams came knocking and as I began what I thought would be another night of fighting, I felt Anthony next to me and thanked God that I would not go through this alone.

In the time of trouble
He shall hide me

Chapter
Four

   Standing solemnly, with my head raised to heaven,
I let the rising spirit of worship engulfing Triumph to
take me in. The gold and crystal chandeliers emanated
amazingly bright lights that shimmered proudly against
the stained-glass windows that relayed stories of salvation, restoration and deliverance. Triumph did not look
like the small wooden church I would visit with my aunt
in Goulds, Florida. There were no Sunday school atten-
dance banners on the wall, there were no wood tithes
and offerings counters. Triumph was the interior designer's version of the heaven scripted in Revelation. Marble
floors with specks of gold, gold trimmed base boards,
lavish cushioned royal chairs lined both sides of the long
foyer. The foyer led to heavy oak doors trimmed in gold,
with gold handles shaped into angels. Once inside you
stepped onto plush carpet, just a shade or so darker than
the deep royal blue pews. The pulpit area covered in silk
flowers, gold and marble end tables sat next to what I
called the Pastor's throne. The ark of the covenant sat
encased before the sacred desk. As you looked around the

room the designers plan to implement royalty, power and strength was evident.

Triumph was also different in that the head deacon did not stand before the congregation and ask for $20 more dollars to meet the needs of the church that week. At Triumph, depending on the occasion we would often do money lines. One line for those who could do a sacrificial offering of $500. One line for those who could do a sacrificial offering of $200 and on and on. I remember thinking one day that there really was no difference in the purpose, the difference was in the approach. I also remember thinking that the money lines are certainly an interesting thing and to me somewhat contradictory. I mean if you give when the line that you can handle is called for, as opposed to when the prayer of offering is raised - then are you giving out of not wanting to embarrass the person that called for the line? I have never bothered to ask anyone about that. It is simply one of those church traditions that I often ponder. Besides, my grandmother always said that "just cause the Lord don't lead you one way, don't mean he don't lead somebody else. Now mind your business."

I took in the high worship and enjoyed the praise from the pulpit. The pounding rhythm of the band complimented the melodic voices of the choir on this Sunday morning. There were some mornings when there seemed to be battle raging up there. Either the musicians were playing louder than the vocalists, or the vocalists would not sing in the key that they rehearsed in, and some mornings the band would start playing one thing and the choir would start singing something else. Not today.

Today, they sounded especially comforting to an ear like mine that had heard screams throughout the night. Ears that had been burning from the cries of other people's pains all night, yes, the praise seemed to wash the congestion from my ears. I was glad to be alive, awake and aware on this morning. I especially liked the Donald Lawrence song, When the Saints Go Up to Worship - even the remix by the music director that was selected for the morning. I heard the woman in the pew behind me say that they should do more of his stuff in church, and I agree, there is not much by Lawrence and Tri-city that I have not enjoyed. It was a song that increased the worship experience for me and usually left me in tears.

I looked around the church searching for something. I wanted to look in each face for some type of invitation, some sign ... there had to be some sign from someone. That was my reasoning. The truth is I just wanted something to assure me that I was not about a fry shy of a happy meal. I know that I am an intelligent woman and therefore this nightmare foolishness is working my last nerve. So, I searched the faces like a hound dog on a rancid trail. There was a young couple with three kids, the oldest still sucking a bottle, the youngest waved his little hands and kicked little blue sock covered feet as his mother praised. Nothing. There was the mothers section, big hats, white gloves and sporadic screams of HALLELU-JAH, PRAISE HIM PRAISE HIM; it seemed they had their own choral arrangement going. Nothing. There were the deacons, in first Sunday black standing tall, as though they were the staunchest warriors in the kingdom. Nothing. There was a young man who seemed out of place in church, yet seemed to be interested in what everyone was getting caught up in. Nothing. I re-focused my attention to the praise leaders before my mind again drifted. The dreams could not be haunting me for no reason. I kept telling myself one of these faces; one of these in this church belongs to those nightmares. I didn't really have a basis for that assumption, except this morning, it rang clear in my spirit. And what is revealed to your spirit self, I believe, will manifest.

It seemed funny to me that I was vividly recalling visions and scenes of things that I had no personal knowledge of. These hauntings were not my experience. They troubled me more than I was letting on. Having been raised and thoroughly so in the church, I firmly believe that God brings you through things and to things for a reason. These hauntings were for a reason. Was there something in my family? Was it because of something in Anthony's family? At that moment, it hit me, there is no depth to my knowledge of Anthony's family. There is the aunt and there is Nisa, but where did they all come from?

I know that Ant has two degrees in Electrical and Mechanical Engineering. I know he went to school in Texas. But where does he come from. Funny, but I don't even know if I have ever seen his birth certificate or social security card. No, I told myself, he's not trying to hide them from you, you have just never seen them. I do know his social security number and his birth date. I cannot say that he has actually ever seen mine. I had to have a personal stake in all of this, for these dreams to take me in so powerfully. Whatever they were, whose ever they were, despite God's clear instruction to me, I wanted these dreams gone and neither prayer nor fasting would stop them. I knew I had to find the main character in the story that premiered in my dreams nightly. In my opinion, the three months my nights had suffered through this invasion had been three months too many.

The touch of someone's hands about my waist and a warm kiss on my cheek interrupted my search for a time. Anthony, tired and a few pounds lighter than a month ago, slid into the pew, squeezing his body between mine and that of a somewhat robust woman who really did not seem interested in the importance of a couple worshiping together on Sunday morning. When her attitude awakened Anthony's, I gently stroked his hand and reminded him that I left without him because he tarried on the pillow too long. I clearly understood why and really, I had not made a fuss about it. My new round of nightly visits was causing my poor baby many hours of sleep as well.

There were nights when he literally could not wake me up from the dreams; rather than continue to try, he would simply hold me. He told me one morning that he thought if he let go, the dreams would take me. So, he covered me while I fought. That is what the Bible says husbands should do, cover their wives. Funny, so many couples believe that is only about the financial part. What happens though if he covers you with the money and the rest of you is left open? That is one of the qualities I appreciate in Ant - he covers me completely. After we were married I confessed to him that the first time we prayed together as an official couple, I was so incredibly aroused. He called me sick. I told him that I read somewhere that if your spirit is truly connected with someone, your attraction to each other will be even more incredible than anything you can imagination at times of high religious experiences. Other times, when the nightmares took hold, he would lead me to a warm shower to wash away the sweat that would cause my nightgown to cling to my body. Still, there were times when I would awaken and want to be with him intimately. I had to remember the feel of this love, of his love, to forget the feel of the pain in my dreams.

"I couldn't pull it together this morning baby." Anthony whispered in my ear as the morning announcements were read. "Those dreams are getting longer and we're both sleeping less. Something's got to give baby."

I didn't know what to say, so I said nothing and rested my head on his shoulder.

"We've got to find a way to stop this. What are the dreams about? What's on your mind baby?"

I thought about his question for the longest time; then when he squeezed my waist again I answered him in what I am sure he must have thought was a curious manner. "Ant, I don't think it's what's on my mind. I think it's what's on somebody else's mind and for whatever reason, the Lord has me watching it."

"I'm worried about you and I'd like to know how.... I don't know.... I know we both need to get some sleep."

His eyes were darker than I'd ever seen them. His frame seemed less steady than it normally was. His squeeze on me was more of concern and security than of love and quiet passion. I could not explain what I could not understand and so I rested my head on his shoulder. I felt the woman next to me rise and realized that

the responsive reading was underway. Reading respon-
sively from the 27 Psalms seemed interesting, but it also
seemed to ease the threats laced in the dreams. As the
psalm was read something lifted from my spirit. While the
words of the New King James Version were voiced aloud,
I found clarity in the printed New Living Translation Bible
Anthony held between the two of us.

*Minister — The Lord is my light and salvation;
whom shall I fear? The Lord is the strength of my life; of
whom shall I be afraid"?*

*Congregation — When evil people come to destroy
me, when my enemies and foes attack me, they will
stumble and fall.*

*Minister — Though an army may encamp against
me, my heart shall not fear, though war should rise
against me, in this I will be confident.*

*Congregation — The one thing I ask of the Lord, the
thing I seek most, is to live in the house of the Lord all
the days of my life, delighting in the Lord's perfections
and meditating in his Temple.*

*Minister — For in the time of trouble HE shall hide
me in His pavilion; in the secret of His tabernacle He
shall hide me; he shall set me up upon a rock.*

*Congregation — Then I will hold my head high,
above my enemies who surround me. At his tabernacle*

I will offer sacrifices with shouts of joy, singing and praising the Lord with music.

Minister — Hear, O Lord, when I cry with my voice! Have mercy also upon me, and answer me.

Congregation — My heart has heard you say, "Come and talk with me" and my heart responds, "Lord I am coming."

Minister — Hide not they face far from me; put not thy servant away in anger: thou hast been my help; leave me not, neither forsake me, O God of my salvation.

Congregation — Even if my mother and father abandon me, the Lord will hold me close.

Minister — Teach me thy way, O Lord and lead me in a plain path, because of mine enemies.

Congregation — Do not let me fall into their hands. For they accuse me of things I've never done and breathe out violence against me.

Minister — I had fainted, unless I had believed to see the goodness of the Lord in the land of the living.

ALL — Wait patiently for the Lord. Be brave and courageous. Yes, wait patiently for the Lord.

Without warning, I felt the very life rush from my body and not even Anthony's arm around me stopped my fall. In my semi-consciousness, I could hear and see the ushers rush to my side, a concern washed over the face of one of them and without even a word from her, Anthony took me in his arms and rushed me to an adjoining room. As members of the church's health ministry checked my pulse, my heart, my breathing, my sugar level, Anthony stood by. Tears clung to his eyelids yet did not fall. I always said he was too stubborn to cry about anything or anyone but the Lord, that didn't stop me from loving him with everything I have in me. Anthony wanted his wife back I knew it. He didn't want the woman who was consumed by dreams and too tired to stay awake to avoid them. Now, he couldn't I told myself as I started to cry, want her – not the her whose body had now collapsed in front of him and there was nothing he could do.

I was the woman he had finally given up everything for, that's what he would always tell me. He wasn't a mac daddy, or a drinker, or a drug user – but he always said it's all gone now that I've got you. Lately these dreams were wearing on us. I was edgy. I was becoming obses-sive about not being around people I didn't know. I was searching for faces in dreams that Anthony kept tell-ing me were not real. I was dwelling on the nights that Anthony used to toss and turn and trying to remember the things he would yell out in his sleep. I begged him just two nights ago, to get rid of the bed. "It's the bed baby. It's the bed, we've had it too long." He thought he was losing me and that I was losing my mind. Two people motioned Anthony out of the room and I wondered why no one responded to me yelling and begging them not to make him leave. I could hear voices, asking him a series of questions yet it seemed odd that I did not hear him. Finally, I started to feel better and felt the consciousness completely coming back as I heard a young woman speak to Anthony.

"She's going to be fine, her heart rate is good ... everything is fine, I'm thinking she must have just been overcome or overwhelmed and the rush of adrenaline took her out. She's breathing fine and her pupils are responsive. Just give her a minute."

Coming in and out, I watched as two women walked off and Anthony pulled a folding chair to the door facing the courtyard of the church. Sitting with his head in his hand for several moments, he did not notice me regain consciousness. But the lone nurse who stayed behind did.

"Crystal ... do you hear me? Crystal, you're at Triumph Baptist Church. If you hear me, nod your head or wave your hand."

I did neither; I really didn't feel like moving I felt like sleeping, I felt like sleeping. "I hear you. I hear you. What happened?"

"You passed out at the end of the responsive reading. We don't usually get people falling out then. But I guess there's a first time for everything."

The woman helped me sit up and steady myself. As I caught her face I recognized her as someone I had seen around, a lot, especially if it was something involving Pastor. At Triumph, young women were plentiful. Young women wanting the attention, the affection and several other parts of Pastor T. L. Brighton were even more plentiful. I was sure this young woman, as attentive and caring as she seemed, was one of those "wanting".

T.L. Brighton at the young age of 32 was dangerous. He was young, incredibly intelligent, very prolific and truly well versed in the Bible. He was good-looking and smooth. If he was thirty to forty pounds heavier, he could have easily been mistaken for hip hop artist LL Cool J. He had the uncanny ability to preach the word in such a manner that commanded the respect of the old mothers, yet truly captured the young ... the drug dealer, the professional, the hooker, the single mother ... he had a style. And truthfully his total package was nice.

Women pretended to be his lover, his wife ... many going as far as to name children conceived in moments of passion after him, hoping that somehow that type of demented thinking would attract him. He was dangerous because he was single and he was popular, especially with the ladies.

I also knew from my brief encounters with T.L. that he was not use to rejection. He was more accustomed to a woman thanking him for palming the roundness of her bottom than asking him if that was an accident. My issue, he told me, when I pulled his coat tail about writing his non-existent book, was that I was too hard to let a man get to my softness. His issue, I told him, was he should not have been trying to get to my softness as my pastor in the first place. I did not get any more flowers after that. I got no more catered in dinners. I did not get any additional late night after church calls to make sure I got home okay. I did not want a pastor who was also my lover. To me, that was almost like courting and sexing God. Sick as that sounds, that's what being with your pastor or a pastor amounted to – for me. I just wanted and needed someone to foster spirit maturation - a pastor.

Ant would often tell me about women he had counseled about inappropriate dress, unnecessary behavior - like jumping up and down and being overcome in the spirit, when the Pastor was merely making pre-sermon opening comments, or leaving their children unattended, unfed and unlearned because they needed to be everywhere the Pastor was. You get so caught up in the man, the Pastor; you forget why you are really in church and what ministry is really all about.

This nurse seemed to have the demeanor of one of these women. It is a demeanor you cannot really describe; it is more of a feeling. The feeling of love when they look at him. The feeling of chastisement when he preaches a text on sanctification. The feeling of anger when word gets out that marriage may be looming for him.

"Where's my husband?"

"He's right outside, sitting. He has not gone off to far."

"That's my Anthony. I've seen you around a lot. Thank you. What's your name?"

"Cathy. Cathy English. I've been a member here for about three years."

"Oh, okay. Am I discharged?"

"Just stand up slowly and when you're on your feet take a few deep breaths and give yourself a moment to adjust."

As I went about the business of following the nurse's directions, I noticed the nurse seemed to be pensive and needed to say something.

"What's wrong? Please don't tell me my dress was up over my head or something. That's all I need; for the saints to notice I was wearing my husband's favorite drawers this morning." Ant has a pair of blue boxers with brown teddy bears all over them, now I was sure some woman had bought them for him, mainly because they were not his style and he never wore them. Teasing him one day, I put them on and he laughed and told me "and just think I was going to throw them away. I guess I'll hold on to them for a little while longer."

Cathy laughed. I watched her cautiously, laughing as well.

"When you get some time, do you think I could talk to you about something? I know you're a writer and I was hoping you might be able to help me with something."

"Something like what?" I checked my dress, hair, and make-up trying to get a handle on my appearance as Cathy busied herself around the room. "Something like what?"

"I need to get my sister and I need you to help me."

"Get your sister from where and how can I help you with that? You need a letter or some type of presentation?"

"No. I need my sister. And every time I think about it lately, you're the first face I see. I need her, before they totally destroy her and I need you to help me."

"Who are they? And what are you talking about?"

"First Born Alliance Holiness Church of the Living God. They are a cult. And I was with them, until I took... here's my number, please, please call me. There's your husband."

Anthony held me for what seemed like forever and that was fine with me. There was after all always something about the feel of that man's arms around me that brought me comfort and joy. We started to walk out of the room, when Anthony suddenly shivered and stopped.

"What's wrong Ant?" I asked him as he turned to face Cathy.

"Where do I know you from?" He asked the question with an unusual manner of distaste, not at all anything like the Anthony I know. Cathy would not look at him in the face and I found that very strange.

"I don't think we know each other at all."

"Oh yeah, we do. Something in my spirit just told me we do and it's not just from around here. We do. You and I... hhm. I'll remember later I sure. I do know you."

Anthony looked at me and smiled to reassure me that he did not just a have a moment of insanity, and together we left Cathy staring at the floor. Considering the strange exchange of words between Cathy and I, and Anthony's recognition of her I noticed that something in me had shifted. I had found the face in the crowd that I searched for. Now I needed to figure out what Cathy, her sister, the dreams and Anthony's distaste of Cathy all had in common.

Finally rejoining the congregation, Anthony and I caught the first phase of the tail end of Pastor Brighton's message on the err of oppression in the church. A message he had preached before out of the book of Exodus - something about his final comments during a frenzied whoop stood out.

"So, let's re-cap this thing this morning. I'm telling y'all, especially those of you visiting and those of you without a church home, don't let nobody get up in the pulpit or stand up professing to be teaching the word of God and tell you that you have to be a slave to a master – who is a human man or woman - in order to worship God. Your enslavement is to the life of Jesus Christ, you strive, you grow, you desire, you long to be like Jesus the Christ, but you don't let nobody tell you that in their oppression of you or in the gutless manner of applauding the oppression of other people that there is God in that. The devil is a liar.

Paul said give up the things of this world; do not be mindful of the things of this world, but press towards the mark of the high calling. When you're pressing, you can't step on other people, when you're pressing you can't beat the life out of someone else that is not where you are in this walk. When you're pressing … you can't get so heavenly minded that you snatching the spirit out of someone else on this earth. Stop being Pharaoh, while you're trying to be Moses too, that ain't of God, who you serving … who you serving!?

Aah, come on now, somebody needs to be free in here today. Drug users know what I'm talking about. When you get so use to one high, it doesn't get you high any more, but something in you tells you need it, you need it, you need it, got to have it … but you got to have some more too. You are a slave to that drug. Just like in Exodus 1 and 11, when the Egyptians made the Israelites their slaves and put brutal slave drivers over them hoping to wear them down, that's what those narcotics do for you.

The weed says, try the cocaine, you say yes master, the cocaine says try the crack, you say yes master, the crack says try the heroin, you say but master, then the crack says okay – okay –okay, don't try it… but I won't let you feel good no more, go ahead put me on that pipe, smoke me all weekend this time, you won't feel nothing. Now, now, now – the next time the crack says try the heroin, you say yes master, yes brutal slave driver, but some-where in there, good God almighty, something in you says I don't want this no more, I don't want this no more.

And that's why it is so important that we evangelize; that we take our snooty selves out there to the crack den. Cause at one of those moments when that slave driver is telling you to take another hit, and it's about to be the hit that kills ya … something in you is going to look up and see big Brother Parker here walking through that crack house and in your high condition, you gone holler "MOSES…. MOSES…. Deliver me."

Deliver me, those were the words that sprang forth each time the hauntings came upon me. Deliver me. Brighton's voice echoed in my mind, just as my eyes caught those of Cathy's. She stood there; clutching her Bible to her chest, one hand pounding on the pew in front of her, her eyes fixed on me. Deliver me.

Tell Jesus
they need deliverance

Chapter Five

In a modest Afro-centric apartment overlooking a modest South Florida community, Cathy dug through boxes of papers, photos and letters. She kept telling herself there must be something here, something that would help her convince Crystal, something that would help her. There was something. There had to be. Some letter, some newspaper clipping ... some church program ... some ministry lesson. Surely there was something in one of these boxes that would corroborate her story. Why would Crystal believe that she had once belonged to a church that had become nothing more than a haven for sexual activities reminiscent of a porn movie, and a Mecca of welfare subsidized living. It was everything Pastor Brighton had talked about in his sermon. Sexual oppression. Religiously controlled-oppression. Financial oppression. It was rape, adultery, child molestation; the epitome of perversion all approved and regulated through the twisted teaching of Rev. William Thompson.

Cathy wondered aloud what Crystal would think of Rev. William Thompson. He was, and still is a good-looking man. When she first met Rev. Thompson she was 12, her grandmother was struggling financially and emotionally. They visited the church because her grandmother believed in going to church on Sunday. His teaching focused on strengthening families. He had a heart for children. "He had a hard on for children." Cathy yelled the words to no one in particular.

There it was. Finally, something to back her up. A simple flyer that encouraged the community to visit the:

First Born Alliance Holiness Church of the Living God,
offering a better way,
we are the church that cares.
Brothers and sisters-
The Lord and we- invite you to start a whole new life.
Attend our worship services at the Lee Elementary
School. Scheduled meetings:
Sunday school .... Sunday 10:00am;
Morning Worship .... Sunday 11:30am;
Christian Education and Prayer Services.... Wednes-
day 7:30pm.
Support a cause that promises a better today and a bet-
ter future for you, your family and your community.

Amid a loud, uncontrollable laugh, Cathy was in tears. "A better today and a better future. God, it still hurts so bad; it still won't go away."

"Hey girl, you cooked all this food for it to sit on the stove and get cold?"

Anthony in his work-out shorts and Cowboys jersey was obviously settled in for the evening. And since there were no games on, football season having just ended, his plan - I could tell from his frequent trips to the kitchen - was to chill with me. But my mind was filled with the conversation I and Cathy had earlier, so I did not hear him. "Crys, baby. Crystal! Crystal. Baby where's your mind? I'm talking to you, woman."

"Come here boy," I pulled my husband to the reading chair next to the kitchen window where I sat, placing his head ever so gently in my lap. "What does my baby want?"

"Right now, I want to know what's going on with my wife. I want to know what takes you away from me at the drop of a dime."

"I'm sorry baby, I know I must seem like I'm losing my mind. These nightmares are driving me crazy. And then that Cathy English lady. There was something – I don't know – weird, maybe unsettling is a better word, about her. Freaked me out."

"What did she tell you?"

"I don't remember everything, I was still a bit out of it and distracted by the fact that she kept moving. Something about her sister and some group…"

"I don't get a good vibe from her Crys. She's not quite settled in the head. Her foundation shifts a lot." He rose and walked over to the refrigerator, looking for nothing, just holding it open. I rose behind him and checked the pots to make sure I hadn't left anything turned up too high and that the oven was on warm and not 450 degrees. Anthony's right, I was easily distracted lately.

"You've talked to her before?"

"After that day, I spoke with one of the ministers about her. She gets offended when she thinks Pastor preached about something in her personal life. Says stuff like she thought it was between the two of them."

'They're seeing each other?"

"Oh, no; at least not in the real world."

"Ant, I'm just going to say this, no prefacing, nothing – I'm just going to blurt it out."

"You know I haven't eaten yet. I don't like bad news on an empty stomach."

"I think that I've been called …."

"To preach?"

"Oooh that would be something, me preaching … no, besides I'm sure Pastor Brighton wouldn't let me in his pulpit."

"Because of your relationship with him?"

"It never was a relationship, hold up - how did you know about that?"

"He told me in a roundabout way one day, a while ago."

"What did he say? If you don't mind you my asking."

"Said he was thinking about taking more aim at that game. I told him it wasn't necessary, I already had you."

"Ooh. What else did he tell you?"

"Nothing I was concerned about. Man, talking to a man about the one he didn't get - that's all. Just for the record, it bothers me that you never told me."

"I guess I figured it was a moot point. He asked, I said no. Moment over. Besides I really didn't want you thinking you were seeing someone that was one of Brighton's ladies. I did not Ant, did not sleep with him. I guess I still should have mentioned it. I'm sorry."

Ant kissed me tenderly and raised by face to meet his eyes. "It's okay. You're where you're supposed to be. So, you've been called...."

"Yeah. I've been called for something. Baby, you know how it is when something just takes over your thoughts and you know that there's some reason..."

"You think those dreams are what, something you need to follow up on."

"Yes, I do. I think I may have stumbled on to something. No actually, I think I've gotten a writing assignment from God himself."

Anthony started doing that quick pace thing he does when he's deep in thought. I have seen him do circles in one place for close to an hour when there is a component in a project that just is not fitting right. I watched him grow more anxious by the second in his pace, in his muscles flinching, in the way he was making points by jabbing things with his finger.

"Crys, I am not liking where this is about to go. I don't know what you're going through woman. But I do know how you get when you get that obsession thing. And I am scared that this is about to be one of those things."

"Am I really that bad?"

"Woman you had me take apart the dishwasher to figure out where one little stream of water came from, because you did not think that water needed to come from there."

"Come on now, you were just as curious as I was, not a good example."

"We took the dishwasher apart woman, and a whole dishwasher later you decided that it was probably all right to begin with. Every time you get obsessed, it costs me money and this one does not feel good to me baby. On a serious tip, it does not feel good and I am not talking about money. Leave this alone woman, just leave it the hell alone!"

Anthony's walking away and getting so serious at a light conversation worried me. Even more importantly, it made me remember that Anthony was all too familiar with what I am going through because he had been there. While he chose to pray the nightmares away; I chose to run to them and figure out what they wanted. He was right; these night-mares, the hauntings, did not feel good. As I slowly placed my arms around him, my fingers lightly combing the hair on his chest, I rested my head on his shoulder blade and tried to re-assure him. When I did, there was a flash in my memory. One night as he tossed in bed, Ant accidentally threw me to the floor. He did not know and I do not recall ever telling him. But right after that, I heard him saying something like ... not another person, you cannot keep this... or keep her... or something ... she is not dead. I knew now, to some degree, that whatever had troubled his spirit had now invaded mine.

"I don't know what the nightmares are about. I prom-ise you I will try not to get obsessed. But I have to figure it out; otherwise it is not going to leave me alone. Be patient with me, okay."

"Crys look baby..."

"Un unh, you don't need to plead your case."

"I'm worried about you girl. You don't know how much I love you..."

"Come on let me feed my man." I loosened the grip of the apron around my waist and let it fall to the floor.

"What did you cook?" Slowly but I assumed willing to be distracted from another argument about something we both were avoiding, Anthony pulled me to him, running his fingers along the crease in my back.

"It won't matter for a few hours." And it wouldn't. For right now all that mattered was the warmth of his lips around my nipples and the strength of his arms as he pulled me about his waist. "Have mercy. Just how hungry are you?"

I felt my body warming, not from my husband's passion - that had already led me in to a deep sleep - for a while anyway. The warming was the sensation I felt each time the dreams; the hauntings came to visit. I tried to wake myself, but I could not. I tried to pull myself away from the hauntings, but could not. And they started, except this time; it was just the faces. The sturdy yet defeated face of the tall, lanky brother. The sweet but very mature face of the angel in the dress. The tear covered face of a mother in a coffin, her daughter and son with tears of blood soaking their face, staring down at her. And there were the black, patent leather shoes and the face of a middle aged, very handsome man who extended his arms in a welcoming fashion. The mother in the coffin rose, looked around at someone. I realized that someone was me. And the mother said, "Tell Jesus. Tell Jesus I waited for deliverance."

The smooth dark skin on the hand of the brother in the shiny leather shoes, struck the mother's cheek. She fell back into the coffin and as the pain became fresh again for her two children they began to cry and the man in the shiny leather shoes held them saying "don't cry; your mother provoked evil. I am your truth and your light." He led the children away from the coffin, seemingly unaware of me, who stood there observing the scene as a stranger. I approached the coffin slowly, realizing that the mother was not dead, but made to pretend to be, or maybe she was dead pretending to be alive. "Tell Jesus," she said, almost wailing, "they need deliverance. Please tell him." Then her face became recognizable, it was Cathy English. Without warning, the coffin door slammed shut and the mother yelled again, "Tell Jesus".

I sat up in bed, realizing my body again was wet with the heat of the hauntings. Letting the water from the shower beat on me, I thought about the dreams and who was this man professing to be Jesus. Was he the leader of the cult Cathy spoke about? What kind of evil did this mother provoke? What did Cathy mean when she said she had to get her sister? Why did she think I could help her do it? While I understand completely that God works in His own way, why were the visions so terribly disturbing?

Shortly past three in the morning, and I was wide-awake. The moments of slumber I had experienced drifted away. My mind was full of thoughts. The image of the man professing to be Jesus invaded me. Opening the Bible that Anthony kept atop his desk, I flipped to the subject index in the back, searching for passages on false prophets or false gods.

"If a prophet, or one who foretells by dreams, appears among you and announces to you a miraculous sign or wonder, and if the sign or wonder of which

he has spoken takes place, and he says, Let us follow other gods" (gods you have not known) "and let us worship them," you must not listen to the words of that prophet or dreamer. The Lord your God is testing you to find out whether you love him with all your heart and with all your soul. It is the Lord your God you must follow, and him you must revere. Keep his commands and obey him; serve him and hold fast to him. But a prophet who presumes to speak in my name anything I have not commanded him to say, or a prophet who speaks in the name of other gods, must be put to death." You may say to yourselves, "How can we know when a message has not been spoken by the Lord?" If what a prophet proclaims in the name of the Lord does not take place or come true that is a message, the Lord has not spoken. That prophet has spoken presumptuously. Do not be afraid of him."

The scriptures banded together to form their own instructions. There was definitely a Word. I pondered on just how plentiful false prophets and false gods could be especially in the black church. Still, the church has changed. It is a conversation I and Anthony entertain several times over.

"They rejected his decrees and the covenant he had made with their fathers and the warnings he had given them. They followed worthless idols and themselves became worthless. They imitated the nations around them although the Lord had ordered them, "Do not do as they do, and they did the things the Lord had forbidden them to do."

I did not notice Anthony standing at the doorway watching me flip from passage to passage. When I paused, placing my glasses on the open Bible and the multiple notepads, he walked over to the chair in front of me.

"Anthony, what if I told you I think those dreams have to do with false prophets and some kind of cult activity."

"What makes you think that? And what kind of cult?" Anthony twisted his head side to side and drew his lips together tightly. This was a conversation he did not want to have in the middle of the night. A conversation was not what he woke up looking for. Knowing his moves, I knew he was hoping he'd find me in the shower, which means the erotic air that delayed dinner could - maybe -might delay breakfast as well.

"I don't know. I told you about Cathy English, the nurse that helped me at the church and how she asked if I would help her find her sister. She was talking like this sister was in trouble..."

"Cults? Crystal what are you walking into? And please do not tell me this has anything to do with that English woman. I've already told you she is not quite complete in the mental capacity area."

"Baby, I'm not walking into anything. But between the dreams and what little information she did throw at me, that's starting to come back to me, I know there's some kind of connection."

"Let's just say there is." The pacing had begun again and this time I watched him intent on trying to see if there was any recognition in anything I was throwing at him. While the anxiety and tension in his body was evident,

Ant maintained his composure to a degree. "What cult are you talking about and what do you figure the connection is? You don't know what you could be getting into with Black cults or any other cults. I mean some of these groups are very dangerous baby. Yahweh Ben Yahweh. Some of them are based in extra-terrestrial and dysfunctional heritage theology like Malachi York and the United Nuwaubian Nation of Moors."

"Yahweh, they were pretty big at one time, right? Malachi York, I've seen his books in stores before. But Yahweh was here in Miami, right?" I grabbed a pad and began to scribble notes again.

"I know they had residential compounds in several places, they used to have a thriving business or two here – and then there was a whole raid or something. But that can't be the group she's talking about. He's been in jail for quite some time. What are you not telling me Crystal? What cult did she mention to you?"

"I didn't write down the name when she mentioned it. But it was something like First Holiness Church of God." If the name meant anything to Anthony, I couldn't tell because he turned his back to me and stared quietly at the Mobassi painting that hung to the right of his desk. "But you know what's strange is a cult that mentions the name of God, isn't that unusual?"

"No not at all." Anthony now seemed to be bothered by the conversation. "I'm not really sure. But, if you are a false prophet what better way to pull people in than with the name of God. I don't think I've ever heard of a church with that exact name. I've heard of something close to it."

"Well it may not be the actual name. I want to call her Ant. I want to call her and find out what she's talking about?"

"Crys, if she is or was in a cult, and she's given you the impression that her sister is in danger, what would make you think I'd let you get mixed up in this?"

"Because you love me. Because you want these dreams to go away as much as I do...."

"Even more."

"And because I think there's a story here. Even more importantly, I think you and I both know that there is something God wants out of this."

Anthony's non-response left me a little tense. His extreme displeasure about this whole matter was now very evident, it, in fact it filled every inch of the room. I watched him begin a slow, short distance pace between the window and the desk. I knew without a doubt his silence meant many arguments. That would have been fine if I really did know what I was walking into.

"What were you researching?" Anthony finally spoke but he continued his pacing.

"Looking at scriptures on false prophets and false gods."

"False prophets come in many forms baby. There are some Baptist, Protestant, and AME false prophets. The church allows and accepts so much now; we laugh about things we know are wrong. We train people to justify sin rather than repent and look for deliverance."

"Ant if you believe that, why go to church, why do we worship?"

"Because baby, you have to know God for yourself. You have got to know Him even when carnality is rampant in the house of worship. In the face of accepting things, you know the Bible speaks against – you have got to have your own knowledge and a true understanding that comes from Him first. You have to see a bigger picture. Think about it. Both your mother and grandmother come from holiness churches. They would never worship at Triumph. We're free yes, but are we so free that we allow things to go on under the banner of freedom, rather than wearing the banner of righteousness and sanctification? If you're looking for the real stuff, a real relationship with Christ, then I shouldn't have to continue escorting you out of the church because of your messed up thing for the Pastor."

"I don't get it. Ant, where is all of this coming from? It sounds like there are some things going on that you're not happy about."

"I haven't said anything to you, but I'm really thinking that Triumph isn't where we need to be. When being free means, you turn your face when or while the man of God has his episodes of.... let's call it ... indiscretion; you should start to question yourself. When it gets to the point that your family, your business, your job, your health suffers because you are running after things of the church and not of God, you get concerned. When you are encouraged to be at everything, condemned when you are not and then receiving the Word of God becomes a secondary bonus to being there, there is a problem."

"Ant, what are you talking about and what are you walking in to?"

"It's like the nurse you're talking about, her name is Cathy, right?"

"Yes."

"I told you I asked around. She is one of the special cases Pastor's staff and security is instructed to watch out for. She has not actually approached Pastor, but her letters and her gifts indicate her imbalance."

"Why are you talking like a cop? Her imbalance..."

'Some of these people baby, we do actually investigate. Be careful, I'm telling you I know this woman from somewhere. This woman has a problem with distinguishing what is real from what is never implied. If she belonged to a cult, you need to be concerned with whether; it was all in her head. You need to be concerned with whether she's just not looking for new members. Let's go to bed. I've got an early morning."

"Are you serious about leaving Triumph?"

"I'm thinking on it. In everything you're reading, you'll find that cults are just an extreme version of spiritual bondage – but they are both corporate methods of worship. Let's just give it a little time. Maybe I'm just tripping."

"Ant is there anything you remember in the nightmares you used to have?"

"No, not really. Every now and then in quiet moments, I see something here and there that kind of rings familiar but strange."

"Like what?"

"Like faces of people I don't know. Dark roads and lots of trees, but I'm awake, so I don't know. Maybe I've just been around that vivid imagination of yours too long."

"Funny." I yawned and had to admit that I was very sleepy. "I guess we can at least sleep until the sun comes up."

"Or we could just find something else to do until the sun comes up."

The phone rang for what seemed like an eternity and my stomach bubbled with anticipation. Why was I so nervous about a simple phone call? The answer simply was this was a call that would mean more arguments with Anthony and the further stirring of my insatiable curiosity. I had been rehearsing what I would say in this call like a scared little mama on her first possible-booty call. Would I say something stupid? Would I give up too much information on the first call? Would I remember to get all the pertinent information on the first call to find out if he was, as my cousin Karen used to call it, passion mark material. I needed to know if Cathy English was in fact buck wild crazy or worthy of a little investigative reporting. Finally, I heard the receiver pick up.

"Hi Cathy, this is Crystal Houston. Listen, I've been thinking about what you said to me the other day. Why don't we sit down and talk? You have any free time today?"

"Sure. Should I come to you?"

"No. Meet me at the North Dade Regional Library, NW 27 Avenue and 183 Street, about 12:00."

"Okay, that's not a problem. Why'd you change your mind?"

"I actually have not. I'm just curious about how you think I can help you."

Searching the Internet, I found sketches of information on various cults. The Nation of Yahweh, who listed

the Crucifixion, not as Jesus' death at Calvary but as
the conviction of one Hulon Mitchell Jr. alias Yahweh
Ben Yahweh, on November 7, 1990. Members of this
group had supposedly been involved in murders and
the removal of body parts of Yahweh opponents, former
members, traitors as they were labeled, and others.

The leader, who the group believed was the true son of
God, was released from prison in 2001 after serving time
in upstate New York. He was loosely convicted of ordering
his members to murder about 14 people in South Florida
between 1992 and 1993. The court in allowing his release
forbids him to have any contact with members of the
church. Yet his children are still active participants in the
group and they in fact host an active website, condemning the government for its errant, racist and hedonistic
crucifixion of their leader. They also produce a weekly
cable television show proclaiming among a litany of misguided teachings, that the white man in America is the
beast and the Black man is the only true heir to God.

Then there was The United Nuwaubian Nation of
Moors, who worship the one chosen one, better known
as Malachi Z. York, who professes to have become part
of this world in a comet in 1970. York also professes to
be an extra-terrestrial; this I thought to myself, is the
brother from another planet, a being from the 19th galaxy
called Illyuwn. He also claims that the Nuwaubian's are
also Washitaw Indians, linked to or descendants of the
Mount Arafat Embassy of the Yamasee Native American
tribes of the original Cherokee, Seminole, Creek, and
Shushuni tribes. They speak two languages, Yamasee and
Nuwaubic.

Dr. York is facing major jail time for escorting under-age girls and boys, including at least one of his wives' children across Georgia state lines for purposes of a sexual nature. While membership has dwindled, those that remain in the group, are fighting for his release. They say the charges were created by evil minds and that York cannot be held because he is not a citizen of this country nor this planet. Part of their belief is in the existence of extra-terrestrial life. They also teach, according to one website, that we will be claimed again via spaceship and not in the coming of Christ.

The more I read through the research, the more websites I dug up, the more frustrated I became. What is wrong with the Kingdom that all of this could be going on and none of us is crying out? To my surprise, one organization listed the Rastafarians as a cult religion as well. Though they didn't specify their reasons; beyond their belief that Haile Selassie, emperor of Ethiopia, was proof of Revelation 5: 2-5, ***"Who is worthy to break the seals on this scroll and unroll it...but one of the 24 elders said to me, stop weeping! Look, the lion of the tribe of Judah, the heir to David's throne has conquered. He is worthy to open the scroll."*** Selassie was and is the King of kings, Lord of lords. Though a sub-culture of Jamaica, many are rejected for their affiliation with The Rastafarian movement. Some Rastafari teach that Christians are not the children of God, because they are not forsaken by their mother and father.

The Peoples Temple was listed because of the large number of African American members. Wow – I felt a major wave of sarcasm washing through me – if being a white pastor over a large mostly Black congregation was all it took to be listed as a cult on this website – then if we went any further on the site I would surely find several churches in South Florida and other cities, including a major one I watch on TV quite often.

I remember as a young child hearing the Jim Jones story unfolding on the nightly news. My neighbors were from the South American nation now made infamous and I remembered asking them if anyone in their family had died. Jones, who allegedly modeled his teachings after Father MJ Divine, led his followers out of this country and in to Guyana. Once there, there were episodes of shootings of alleged defectors. There was also a well televised service of peace; a service where parishioners were told that they were ready for life abundantly with the Father. The twisted lesson on peace leaving the world shocked and aghast when thousands of members drank a Kool-Aid like beverage laced with cyanide.

Jones' whole ministry grew in inner cities and primarily Black neighborhoods. Some psychological studies on the cult, surmised that Jones was not welcomed in Anglo communities because of his ultra-charismatic, ultra-Pentecostal style. But because he resembled old fashioned whooping Black preachers, people of color flocked to him. He preyed on people that were economically down-trodden and socially defeated, promising better life, and glorious blessings. Behind the scenes, he reportedly reined with iron fists and a do or die mentality. The same character summarization was common with all of these guys, Yahweh, York, Selassie, and Jones.

Before I realized it, it was 11:35 and I was running late for my meeting with Cathy. Scrambling about the house grabbing notepads, purse, keys, I glanced a note sitting on top of the TV. Picking it up, I felt a bit more apprehensive. The note read, **"Be careful, false prophets come in various packages. I love you woman, Ant."**

She has become the
hide-out of demons

Chapter Six

I was getting antsy. I hate being late, but I really hate waiting for people who also were late. Thirty minutes had gone by. I had already waited for ten minutes outside, watching the runners begin their slow trot from the library parking lot along the path adjacent to the library. I watched mothers with their little ones close by wander through the library doors, I assumed for kiddie reading time. Then I decided the heat was growing uncomfortable and I would use the cool air and stillness of the library as the backdrop to formalize my thoughts. Once inside and since I was stuck here staring at my watch every two minutes, I decided to do some additional research on this whole black cult issue.

What made a group a cult? Several things: communal living, the requirement to separate from family, friends, acquaintances, the requirement not to release any information about the church, in many instances – requiring members to change their names and personal identification, the presentation of a doctrine where the leader is placed next to or above God or Jesus or proclaims to be the one true God or son of God. How do you end up in a cult? Cults seem to prey on young people who are going through emotional and psychological stress, people who are disgruntled or disillusioned by their worship experience, and they prey on cultural strengths, like touting that one race of people is superior to all others, according to the Bible.

Looking through a row of books, I noticed Cathy burst into the library. She literally burst through automatic sliding doors like a kitten being chased by great danes. She looked frightened and terribly apprehensive, looking all around like there was a mob of hunters that she had to hide from. She had this look like a little girl playing "I'm invisible", like if I look like nobody seems me, then maybe nobody does. I watched her momentarily, trying to figure out just what was wrong with her. No one was following her and she didn't seem to be hurt. She was just, as my friend Maggie called it, spastic – frazzled – all over the place. Finally, I waved her over to my spot in the library.

"I'm sorry I was late. I started having second thoughts you know. But then I couldn't just leave her there you know."

"No I don't. And you have nothing to have second thoughts about. Is there something wrong? You seem kind of anxious maybe even scared."

"No. Nothing's wrong. Pastor Thompson is a powerful man, if he knew I went to anybody, he would find me." She again looked around to see if the eyes were on her and so I looked around as well.

"How long have you not been a part of Pastor Thompson's church?" She opened a notebook and slid out a stack of papers and then slid them back into the notebook quickly.

"About four and a half years."

"You do know, that if he's powerful enough to make you think he'll come looking for you, he could have already found you if he wanted to." She fumbled through her purse pulling out three or four pens, staring at them, shaking her head as though she spoke to them and then put them all back in her purse. I discreetly tried to notice the other contents in her purse because surely there was some type of medication she forgot to take.

"He has a lot of members and friends here; he may already know where I am. I don't care. I just want to get my sister out of there."

"And how do you think I can do that? Why do you think I would?" The notebook once again discarded the pile of papers and what appeared to be newspaper clippings and just like before it sucked them back in.

"My mother died when I was 14. My father beat her to death. Two months after the funeral I went to stay with my grandmother in Philadelphia. When my aunt here in Miami got sick we moved back to take care of her and my cousin. She belonged to First Born Alliance Holiness Church of the Living God and since it was a rule in my grandma's house that we went to church, we joined."

"Your aunt and her family belonged to the church, so was there an indication that anything was wrong?" This time I pulled the papers away from her when the notebook dejected them yet again.

"No not at first. By the time we got here, she was really sick and my grandma was just trying to hang on. My aunt was dying, that meant both her daughters; both her children would be dead within a year. So, if there was anything strange we didn't notice it. So anyway, after my aunt died, it was just grandma, James and me. We got really involved in the church. James and I would go to Pastor's house a lot because he had kids our age, and because, for all the kids in the church it was a treat to go to Pastor's house." She pulled a small flyer from the stack of papers laid it on top and tapped it, then began her look around the library for the seventh time.

"How many kids does he have and I'm assuming he's married?" I looked around the library again as well. I wanted to see the spirits that were troubling her.

"He has four no five, four boys, uhm five daughters, uhm and yes he's married. After about two years, my grandmother died. James and I were just messed up. I didn't know where my father was. James hadn't seen or heard from his father since his mother's funeral. By this time, James was 18 so he joined the service. I remember him telling me to find my dad and go to him. Don't stay here. But I wasn't going to my father even if I did find him; he killed my mother. He told me he didn't mean to … but still …I found out years later that he, (James) and Pastor had a major fight about him going to the service. Then I thought about it … when James signed his enlistment papers he never went back to Pastor's house, that's where we were staying. He never went back."

'Why didn't he go back?"

"He never told me. I was never allowed to get any of his letters. Pastor Thompson and his wife told me there was no reason to communicate with him, if he was concerned about me and what happened to me, he would have stayed like a man of God and took care of his family, me. He chose to cast his self away from his treasure, he became known as the prodigal son in the church. I kept waiting for him to come home."

"Where is he now?"

"He is still a military man, married, kids, lives in Hawaii. I saw his name mentioned in an article or something and called him. We talk every now and then."

"So why won't he help you get your sister? And why has there been no sister in this story you're telling me."

"Glenice became my sister by way of adoption in the church. Pastor Thompson said I needed someone to grow up with. He partnered most of the girls up like that. But different things happened and Glenice ended up at the church in Ohio and I ended up in New Jersey."

"If you just left, why can't she?"

"I didn't just leave. I got hurt and had to be rushed to the hospital. When the mother walked off to go check in with the Pastor, I ran, hid beneath a train station for two days and then hitched rides back here. I just … I've always felt like I abandoned her."

"What was going on? What would make you run away from a church? And why do you feel like you abandoned her?"

"I can't tell you that. I brought these for you," she pulled more clippings from her purse. This conversation was tiring me out, she had papers in a notebook she wasn't sure she wanted to let go of. She had clippings in her purse as though she was hiding them from me and she cannot decide how many kids this man has or their sexes. Unstable, I thought is not an accurate word to describe this woman. "A couple of newspaper clippings, and some letters Glenice and I would write to each other. We never thought it was safe to talk to each other, in case, somebody was listening. I really gotta go. I hope you'll help me."

"What's your religious experience now?"

"I'm a member of Triumph."

"That's not what I asked you. I asked you what your religious experience is. Do you proclaim that God is the head of your life, or is it Pastor Brighton? Is your understanding of doctrine alright and do you have anything to do with First Alliance now?"

"Look just know that I love the Lord. I really need to go now."

"Wait a minute ... wait a minute. You give me a quarter of a story, make me pull some papers out of your hands, get nervous when I question you about your relationship with God and you expect me to go off and be your super hero or heroine as it is? How about you just report her missing or kidnapped?"

"No! Please. I can't. I really can't. Just look over everything and then, just let the Lord use you. That's all I ask. Revelation 18 and 2 says:

"And he cried mightily with a strong voice, saying, Babylon the great is fallen, is fallen, and is become the habitation of devils, and the hold of every foul spirit, and a cage of every unclean and hateful bird."

"Your invitation to a fallen city like that is not appealing. I'll read the stuff, but there is something you're not telling me and whatever it is, I'll have to know before I agree to do anything. Are you still involved with Thompson and First Alliance?"

Her mood grew angry and once again her movements were frantic. The final question had struck a chord. As she walked away from me barely balancing the contents of her purse, the purse itself and her notebooks, she growled her bothered response.

"I, Mrs. Houston, am not involved with anyone." Then she suddenly changed her mind and sat rather peaceably back at the table where we had been discussing her dilemma.

With that, I gathered up my notebooks, and walked off. Cathy just sat there, dumbfounded, staring at the table. Clearly, I had not responded the way she had hoped I would and she had no conversation or plan to persuade me in this up-in-the-air gesture. There was something evil in what had transpired, or at least the spirit of evil was upon it. Whatever it was, it filled up my guts, turning and bubbling until I left remnants of my breakfast in the library parking lot, calling out for Jesus.

That evening, after giving Anthony highlights of my meeting with Ms. English, he and I went over the newspaper clippings. Clippings that lay amidst collard greens on a cutting board and a roast decorated with lightly browned onions, potatoes and baby carrots. I lightly frosted a yellow cake, while Anthony went about setting the table, occasionally sticking his finger in the can of frosting. There was nothing major in the news stories. But there were indications that something may have been going on. Pastor Thompson and the First Born Alliance Holiness Church of the Living God were being investigated for violations of Child Labor Laws and possible fraudulent use of social security, welfare and WIC benefits.

"So Crys. You've got this stuff, you figure she's keeping something from you, you know already that I think this is trouble. Matter of fact Crys - I know this is trouble."

Ant stared at one clipping in a fashion I cannot even describe. There was familiarity yet curiosity in his eyes. His shoulders, if my eyes were not deceiving me, drooped. That would probably not have caught my attention except it is a position I have never seen in Anthony's demeanor. Shoulders that broad, when drooped, like what I saw before me, seemed quite defeated and overcome. "So, what now baby?"

"Anthony, are you all right?" His response to my question was a simple re-adjustment of his body language. His brief stare in the direction of my face, because it was clear he did not see me at that moment, forced my breaths to become slow and labored. My words had to be deliberate and chosen carefully. "What if one of the guys in the church came to you with something like this, what would you do?"

"Thought out all of your arguments I see. All right baby, we won't argue. What's the plan and what do you want me to do?"

"I want to know what the story with her is. If she's making moves on the Pastor, I need to know why. And I need to know what anybody else knows about her. I don't want any surprises you know. Ant. Where do you know her from?"

"I told you what I know about her already." This time he looked directly into my eyes, intimidating me, begging me to stop the line of questioning before things went too far.

"But where do you know her from baby? I saw the way you looked at her. You know her, don't you?"

"I recognize something about her, that's all. I don't know why. I don't recall ever meeting her. It was just something. That's it on that - all right." He grabbed a handful of grapes from the frig and devoured them quickly. Nerves I thought. Nerves like the ones bubbling in my soul spot as we continued a discussion that only seemed to excite me. "So, you're pursuing this for what reason?"

"False prophets. If there are false prophets, there are false kingdoms. And all those kingdoms must fall. Baby, it's the same thing you were saying this morning, if you see something wrong in the kingdom and you don't do anything...."

"Don't throw my sermons back at me woman. You've read up on some of the cults that exist and have existed, you know that these people can be dangerous. I mean of course they all deny it when they get caught or they justify it in some fraudulent Biblical interpretation; but I need you to understand that this stuff is real. Do you understand that?"

I had seen my husband this worked up in a situation only once before. Kervin Richardson, his former partner, had apparently been embezzling money and Anthony caught it when he hired a new firm to audit their books. Then, like now, his arms were all over the place. He pounded the kitchen counter so fiercely I kept watching his knuckles to see if they were bleeding. He was yelling, strangely not at me, but at whatever was troubling him. I couldn't keep my eyes focused on one thing and so they traveled from his knuckles, to his eyes, to the counter top, to the pots and plates.

"Crys, they will kill you, crazy former members will kill you because they are confused, and reality is non-existent for the people that run these groups. You're potentially walking into a field of explosives and in the meantime, you're asking me to stand by and do nothing, say nothing...""

"I'm asking you to at least trust me enough to look into what's there first. My curiosity has got the best of me."

"Curiosity killed the cat."

"Maybe that cat didn't have a husband to cover her."

"I can only cover you if you let me. I know you woman; don't do anything I don't know about. Crys, there are some things that you just don't understand; some things that you don't know baby. Girl, I am trying to protect you and the best way I can do that right now besides prayer is to tell you to let this go. This is pain for me, understand pain. Let this shit go."

I threw the assorted ingredients for the salad in the bowl nearly missing it because I was now growing tired of Ant's tone. Still I did not respond verbally. As I continued to busy myself about the kitchen, Anthony's pull against the band of my pants stopped me.

"Did you hear me? Nothing I don't know about. Crystal I'm talking to you."

"No actually you're cussing at me."

"That I did. This whole thing girl - is not right - something's up here and ...just don't ... just let me know what you're doing and when you're doing it. You got me?"

"Well then I should tell you something. Come on let's eat."

"Uhn uhn. Tell me on an empty stomach."

"I thought you didn't like bad news on an empty stomach."

"Doesn't matter right now. Just tell me."

"I kind of held back one little clipping I dug up at the library. It's from a local paper. Seems the First Born Alliance Holiness Church of the Living God is holding a revival conference in town next week."

A certain anger and fear washed over Anthony's face. For the first time, I realized that my husband may have been trying to tell me about the things he would call locked away in some kind of sheltered deliverance. Meaning the deliverance had come but what it came from was hidden. I know Anthony well enough to know that pressuring him to tell me what he kept sheltered would not work. He raised his eyebrows physically requesting an answer to his question. "What did you register for?"

"The visitors' session. It's at a hotel baby, place full of people, nothing can happen there."

"You know I'm out of town next week. Crys, this is the very thing I'm talking about, obsession...you don't know jack about these people, but you're going to a damn conference..."

"I'll take Maggie with me, it'll be fine. Ant, please..."

"Maggie ... just in case you haven't noticed is about twelve eggs short of a dozen. And I'm supposed to trust that she's going to watch your back. No Crystal. No. Stay away from them and stay away from that woman until I get back. Look Crys, I know you think I'm just being hard and over-protective. But give me a few days; give me some time to ..."

"To what Ant? What are you talking about now?"

"Look baby girl. Stay away from them until I get back. If you just want to get some information on this church, there's a phone number on my desk for a guy I know that has some information on them. You can talk to him, but that's it Crys. I'm going to trust you – if you believe this is what you need to do. But you gotta trust me too baby. You need to know that ..."

"I need to know what Ant?"

"That this may not be about Cathy English or false prophets at all – at least not in the way you think."

Present your bodies as
living sacrifices

Chapter Seven

I love Crystal. I tell her that every day and I tell every woman that offers me an inappropriate invitation to lunch, dinner, a weekend in the Bahamas – I love my wife. There's no woman that's going to take care of me the way she does. She's ultra-confident in everything she does. She has this natural questioning bug that gets going and she's off head first into some adventure. Our first anniversary, when I should have brought my wife, my jewel – a lovely gemstone or some delicate piece of gold, silver or platinum – I opted instead for two new computers. When she tore off the gold wrapping paper and red ribbons, her eyes lit up and she was giggling. Can you believe that giggling? She was like a little girl in a store with all her favorite dolls and enough money to buy them all.

I must face it; Crystal is going to get into things that I don't know about. She used to tell me about every article she was commissioned to write. We soon realized though that my practicality and my role as protector when placed up against her need for journalistic excitement and danger would often lead us into major battles.

So Crys stopped volunteering the information and I stopped asking.

I cannot tell you how many times I have been sitting in an office or an airport and pick up a magazine only to see an article with her byline. I would swell up with pride and look around with a broad smile. In my mind, I'd be telling everyone - that's my woman's name. See it right there, Crystal Houston - that's my woman. Then, I'd read some of the articles, undoubtedly and often, I would hear myself say these words. "What is that woman thinking? Was she thinking? I'm gonna kill her. I don't know what she's up to now either Lord, so please watch over her while I'm away."

When I first met my jewel, I knew she was the one. We immediately had this very comfortable connection. On our second date, we went to church together, hung out at the beach the rest of the afternoon and went back to church that night. She is something else. She is such con-stant contrast, one minute she's in a black Kenneth Cole dress, trying to get an interview with a drug boy; the next minute, she's in my blue boxers, bare breast in an apron cooking a big dinner in the middle of the week. The whole while she's cooking I'm looming in the kitchen, allowing myself to be aroused and laughing at her daring me to touch her.

Crystal is this butterscotch colored woman with wavy, dark black natural hair and a butt you know you can bounce a quarter off of at any moment. Only one other person had been able to open me up the way Crystal did. That whole relationship and everything that went with it, I keep locked away deep inside.

When Crys and I got married, all of it starting coming up in dreams. All I could do was pray them away and ask the Lord to please just give me the time to deal with it. I should have told Crys about all of it before I married her; but I couldn't risk her thinking that maybe I wasn't the one she should marry. I locked it all inside and purposed that all I had experienced in my past would not destroy what I am blessed with in this woman. Now the dreams are waking up my wife because we have physically and spiritually taken in and on each other's spirit. This time with the nightmares and everything else I know is coming, I may not have a choice to keep things buried. My truth may save or end her life. My truth may end our marriage.

When I was twelve the First Born Alliance took me on the first of what would be many scary trips. I had grown up in this church. I had no father, not that I knew of at the time and the woman I called my mother was also a mother in the church. Whatever Pastor ordered she submitted to and my travels, starting at 12 was one of his orders. Everything I knew about God and families and communities came through that church. We drove over to a large wood multi-frame house that sat a bit off from a highway. It was a southern home in rural Akron. I remember when we got there the sun was setting and the house was surprisingly quiet. A quiet breeze was blowing the limbs of various trees and flowers. That same breeze sent a curtain dancing through the air of one of the bedrooms and it got snagged on this big tall tree.

We walked into this huge front room that looked like something out of an old black and white movie – I knew those movies well because it was all we could watch. I looked around and thought 'ah man, this is tight. I can be all right here.' At twelve, there was a lot I could do with that much room. I could build fortresses. I could build mini-churches and preach sermons like the Pastor did. I could be in my own little world of peace and quiet without any of the other First Alliance kids. Then the peace that filled me about that house and made me feel comfortable and all right - was interrupted by the sounds of items falling and glass breaking.

The deacon that drove me to the house told me to follow him to a room. He said I was old enough to see firsthand, the wrath of almighty God when you disobeyed his commandments. When we walked into this room, the first thing I noticed was these strips – they looked like smaller versions of those sharpening belts barbers used. They shimmered as they smashed against the body of a young woman, and she cried out. The ritual continued for several moments. Intermittently, the voice of an older woman rang out scriptures.

"Therefore, I urge you, in view of God's mercy to offer your bodies as living sacrifices, holy and pleasing to God – this is your spiritual act of worship. Will you worship?" The belt crashed against her yet again. "Will you show reverence to the man of God?" The belt crashed against her yet again. "Will you be a living sacrifice?"

"Please stop." Her voice trembled against the vibration of the belt on her body. Her tears covered her face dripping down onto the arms that tried to hold off the belt from her body. "I am sorry, please forgive me. I'm sorry."

The woman who read the scriptures was Adele Thompson, the wife of Pastor William Thompson and the woman I had grown to call Goddie. Later, I found out that she was supervising was the chastisement of a member who had refused to offer her body for the sexual edification of the Pastor. Beaten and broken she later agreed to provide what she had never given to any other man besides her husband. The husband Pastor Thompson had ordered her to marry at only 14. It was the first time it occurred to me that there was something wrong. I remember asking myself, why would she be beaten for refusing to commit adultery and why would Goddie beat her for not wanting to sleep with my God-father. There was something wrong. I looked up at the deacon who did not seem to be bothered by what was happening. He instead, I remembered, was smiling. So, since it was clear he did not think this was wrong and surely the ones involved did not think this was wrong, I kept my mouth shut. I think I fought back some tears too and for the first time in my young life, I asked God, "what should I do?"

Slowly and methodically the same women who had beaten her until part of her fleshed bubbled as though it had been burned, bathed her. The warm water seemed more painful than anything else. I watched her flinch and tremble so hard you could hear the water stirring – even in that secret viewing closet. Goddie told the women to add the milk bath and a touch of Epson salt for the wounds. While the milk bath and light suds should have soothed her, it really frightened her more and now seeing I and the deacon standing there – he with an air of pride and me just wide-eyed and scared – I'm sure must have added to the horror of her moment.

This was the first time I had seen a naked girl. She had breasts, yes but there were red-striped bruises across them. She had a vagina with wisps of curly black hair, yes, but her thighs were so swollen from the belt that they nearly hid it. She had a small round bottom, yes, but it looked much like her breasts bruised with red stripes. I was afraid. I was terrified of this naked girl in front of me. She was truly scared, more afraid than I had ever seen anyone in my whole life; but she dared not speak. Not with the memory of her first refusal still tingling on her skin. Adele Thompson again spoke to her in a very rude and arrogant tone.

"You are a leader in this church; you should never have had this to happen to you. You know the requirements of young women in this church. You are a leader and let me remind you as you are being prepared that part of your responsibility as a leader is protecting the doctrines and practices of the Pastor."

Naked and shaking Nujima Tahira was led into a bedroom just down the hall from where she had been beaten. As she was escorted past the door of the room, the smell of her sweat and blood still ringing in it frightened her. Though I could tell looking back into her eyes that it caught her by surprise, she knew better than to stop or even slow her pace. I had seen her before, just a couple of days earlier she sat on the porch of Mother Akira's house braiding and platting hair with some of the other young girls.

Most of the girls of at least 13 would begin to frequent Mother Akira's, it was where they learned to be wives and caretakers of the men in the ministry. It was where they learned to handle themselves like ladies. This was one of the young women I watched from the kitchen window, giggling, because I did not know how else to react to the sight of so many pretty girls. My reaction to now seeing one of those pretty girls naked and beaten was not one of humor.

The door to the room opened and two women donning soft white, flowing nightgowns greeted her. The deacon, who had gone ahead of us, had changed into a robe and instructed me to sit in another small closet connected to the room. The closet was just that with a wide glass facing the bedroom, a big black cloth chair, a small table and a box of napkins. The other closet only had a small glass window with a curtain attached to a rod for opening and closing. He said I was about to see the land of milk and honey. What I witnessed was something that gave me my first knowledge of a man's reaction to a woman's body. What I witnessed made me even sicker than seeing Nujma's torn flesh. To this day, I know that it is God's grace which allows me to enjoy the touch, feel, essence and sex of my woman without the horror of the things I've seen crippling my desire.

The women were Adele and Fujana, Pastor Thompson's cousin and the only member of the church who freely traveled. Pastor Thompson sat in a large, burgundy leather chair near the window. A tall man with a large muscular build, he wore his 40 plus years well. Salt and pepper neatly trimmed haircut. A trim-line salt and pepper mustache fell perfectly around his thick lips. I used to see him and think man, when I get to be an old dude, that's what I want to look like. He would always tell Brother Lee to trim it right so that the people would notice his mouth and hearken intently to his words. As he rose, the gold robe about him gave him an immediate air of power and control, and for Nujima fear.

"Sisters, our young lamb has been bruised in the battle. Pour out the oil of joy on her and minister to her accordingly." He raised his arms above his head as he gave his instructions. I stared at him for what seemed liked hours. What was this about? With his tall body standing in front of the window, and the curtains blowing in loops behind him, his arms raised and the setting sun reflecting off his gold robe, he looked like he had just dropped in from heaven.

As I allowed my eyes to fall on the scene that he was watching, I asked myself if this was the nasty behavior Sister Monifa had taught us about in Miami just five days prior. Maybe I should just tell them I want to lie down. Since leaving Miami, the deacon and I had been to New Jersey and now to Akron. Still, after watching what just happened to Nujima, I decided to shut up and watch as I was instructed. And I remember watching and becoming uncontrollably aroused for the first time, yet, feeling ashamed and embarrassed for the girls. I could not figure out what was going on. I had no idea that in some regards you could be aroused and repulsed simultaneously. I did not want to watch that but I liked the tingling that was charging my stomach and my penis. I did not want to watch what was happening but I liked the warmth that was consuming me.

My Godfather would occasionally engage as the two women rubbed oil on Nujima's body; paying special attention to her breast and nipples. They delicately allowed their fingertips to linger along her waist and navel. Her breathing became heavy. Pastor Thompson sat, enjoying the vision before him.

"That's it child, allow this ministry to take over. This is part of your deliverance from rebellion and stubbornness."

The oil dripped from the fingers of the two women along her inner thighs. When they sensed her growing weak, she was led to an overly large bed that sat in the middle of the room. Adele pulled Nujima's oily body atop hers, deliberately yet seductively directing the actions of the young woman. Fujana, in the meantime, stood before the Pastor and disrobed, revealing her young and muscular body. He likewise disrobed and allowed the ministry to enthrall him. Soon, the pairs changed and the ministry continued. I witnessed many other scenes like these over the years. By the time, I was I guess 16 or 17, I was ordered to take part in a couple of special ministry sessions. Sessions where some of the young women that braided hair on the mother's porch, embraced my manhood at my request and allowed me to embrace their womanhood in any fashion I chose. That is where I met the only woman I have loved besides Crystal. That is when I understood the whole transference of spirits during sex thing.

I am sure in any normal situation; I would have wanted to marry her. For my 18th birthday, I was anointed as a minister and a leader in the church; and I could travel with

Fujana. I didn't know why I was chosen to go with her; no other kids had ever had that privilege. One April day as Fujana and I prepared to go to Texas to scout out the land since Pastor Thompson was considering opening another church there, my mother kissed me and hugged me good-bye as she always did. This time however, she did not whisper be a good boy, instead she said - "listen for the voice of God, your deliverance is nigh."

It was then, on that trip, that I came to the truth; that there was no God in what was happening in First Alliance. In traveling with Fujana, there weren't as many restrictions, so I would wait for her to get into one of her ministry sessions, most of the time with men who were not affiliated with First Born Alliance, and I'd sneak out and visit a church, or go to a library and read. The more I read, the more God enlightened me, the more I knew this was wrong. I decided that I needed to figure out a way to leave. I decided to pursue higher education. You see, young people were educated in one of the church locations in Akron or Trenton. If you wanted to go to college, you were shipped to this small school in Miami – where the education was more intense. But you were only allowed to major in things that Pastor thought the church needed. I decided I wanted to major in theology, as one of those anointed by the pastor that was not funny. He expected exceptional performance in class. Strangely, the doctrine and curriculum presented contradicted everything God himself had begun to teach me. Yet, I excelled beyond Pastor Thompson's wildest imagination and I used it to my advantage. With his approval and blessing, I started studying every Bible Pastor would allow me to.

The more I studied, the more I heard the voice of God calling me out and the more I realized that this wasn't just wrong—it was demonic.

Stepping from the shower, I realized that Cathy English's involvement in First Alliance was still very active. There were blocks of time when you wouldn't see her at Triumph and when she would come back – she would seem really depressed and disturbed. The first time I noticed her, I knew the look – I had seen it so often before I got out. But that day in the nurses' room, I couldn't put her face with First Alliance – nor with the periods of disappearance. But it was clear now; something was going on and maybe I should tell Crystal everything tonight, instead of waiting until I get back.

When I stepped into our bedroom, I heard her favorite jazz CD playing and realized she was very soundly asleep. The nights of restlessness had increased so much, that I took the time to enjoy her peacefulness. I adjusted the air conditioner to a cooler 68 degrees, knowing that she undoubtedly would reach for me or the blanket at some point. It's funny, but after five years, she still cannot seem to put her hands on that blanket, but she and those hands always seem to find me. After five years of marriage, I am still thrilled that she looks for that blanket sometimes three or four times a night. Because she does, I am also very spoiled and very satisfied.

I could not wake her, not knowing that sooner or later during the night the dreams would. I climbed into bed next to her and pulled her close to me. Trying not to wake her, I kissed her as softly as I could on the lips and stroked her face, praying that God would release her from the pain of my past and that she would let go of it. She nestled closer to me and through her sleep I heard her say, "I love it."

"I love it too baby girl. And nobody and nothing is going to take it. Sleep well."

Prodigal sheep
going in for the slaughter

Chapter Eight

It was shortly past two in the afternoon and I sat in the middle of the office Anthony and I shared covered in Bibles, notepads, print outs, newspaper clippings. I had a video news clip about the Movement for the Restoration of the Ten Commandments on one computer screen, a shot of Pastor William Thompson on another; and a shot of my boo taped to his leather executive chair. It was my sick sense of humor. I figured if he went ballistic about me going to that conference anyway, I could just tell him – 'you were right there when I faxed it over.'

What I had managed to find out about the First Born Alliance Holiness Church of the Living God was that they were under investigation. Apparently, there had been several "escapes" from the church in the last two to five years, some of those leaving, ended up being interviewed by child welfare services. Much of the information listed a Miami-Dade County investigator, Warren Levy; interestingly, that was also the name of the investigator Ant had on his desk. Why was he interested in First Born Alliance? I made a note to really think about that later, but in the meantime, I assumed that he too had become intrigued by the Cathy English angle. Stay focused on Warren Levy, I told myself and as quickly as I did, I hastened contacting him and arranging a meeting. For the moment, I decided not to tell him I was Anthony's wife.

Levy was a young, sharp man. Jeans and t-shirts, Nikes and baseball caps. He looked like something right off a popular detective show.

"So, Ms. Adams, what's your interest in this case? You have a family member inside or what?"

"No I don't. I'm not sure what my interest is. A young lady at my church belonged to First Born and says she wants me to help her get her sister out. But she's very evasive and I'm not sure she even knows what she really wants."

"And your curiosity has gotten the best of you. When the attorney first called me about this I was like – man, hell NO! I mean, the last thing you wanna do is go messing with a Black preacher. My nanna used to say the next thing to God is the preacher. But there is definitely a Sodom and Gomorrah resurgence going on there."

"So, are they planning to press charges?"

"That's where the drama begins. You see we've got two primary groups of people who have come out of this organization. Older women – who know what they know second hand and aren't talking. The other group is men and women, about our age, who were taking part or forced into some awesome shit – I'm sorry, I'm a cusser."

"It's all right; my husband used to be a cusser too and shit was his favorite word. Since I've gotten into this First Born stuff, it's re-emerging quite frequently. What kind of stuff were they into?"

"That's what I'm not sure of yet. I did meet one guy that gave me some firsthand knowledge of a lot of strange things – that's how I was able to find some other people. Now that guy seems pretty normal. I've tracked down several of them, a couple told me they will not talk. They are afraid of this man. One guy has agreed to meet me – he's scared of this guy too."

"Why do you say that?"

"He lives in Texas now; he wants to meet me in Alabama. Thompson, he told me 'is like a jealous lover ... he doesn't want you back, he just doesn't like knowing you left.'"

Warren, I could tell had really gotten into this investigation. He was happy to share this amazing story with someone. He was obviously good at what he did. His very Art Deco office was adorned in plaques and framed certificates of appreciation. He had an organizational section in his office for each case he was currently working. First Born had a rather expansive area along the wall that led to a large picture window. The window was a beautiful frame of the ocean view. I did not know that there were offices like this on South Beach. As we talked, Warren would reference various sections within the First Born command center and I would follow him my curiosity ablaze.

"The lady I'm talking about, is there any way to find out if she had any special connections in this church?"

"What's her name?"

"Cathy English."

"What was her name in the church?"

"I'm sorry ..."

"Thompson had a nice little racket going, he would give people new names, get social security numbers for them, make them apply for all kinds of federal assistance. That's where the charges are coming from now, looks like fraud or racketeering. Plus, I'm sure once things started getting freaky in the church it helps if you're living under an alias."

"So, he just changed names?" He pointed towards an easel holding a yellow presentation size post-it note pad, titled THE NAME GAME.

"Yeah. The guy I'm going to meet was born Wilbert Anderson, his name in the First Born Alliance Holiness Church of the Living God, was Yahimo Akur. Names don't really mean anything, at least not that my research can show. But again, it's the power thing. I change your name; I mold an identity to go with it."

"So, if I wanted to find this woman's sister, knowing her birth name would do me no good. And she would know that."

"Of course, she would. Some of the people who have gotten out are confused; they are terribly messed up in the head. They hide themselves because they don't know how to live outside. Because of that some went back and it wasn't a pretty sight."

"But if you've found all this out ...."

"I've had tremendous help from the guy I mentioned earlier."

"Maybe I can talk to him too, what's his name?"

"Houston..."

"I'm sorry, what? His name is what?"

"Houston. Can't give you all of his information, sorry." I suddenly started coughing uncontrollably. Why in the hell does Anthony know so much about this church? Why in the hell is he feeding information to this investigator? As I coughed, Warren pulled me into a chair and urged me to take deep breaths. As I did, he wandered off and down a hallway. I had to pull it together, I told myself. Just calm down girl, I said. Maybe you're rubbing off on Anthony for once and he did some research of his own to help end this story quicker. Just calm down. Just as I began to get my natural caramel color back, instead of the tomato red that had suddenly overtaken my flesh, Warren returned with a glass full of ice and a bottle of Dasani water.

"You okay?"

"Yes, I am. You know how you get those tickles in your throat that you hope a cute little cough will take care of and then next thing you know you're about to cough up a lung. Sorry 'bout that and thanks for the water."

"Not a problem, it happens to us all. Anyway, like I was saying, the church is a hard thing to mess with. It's a very fine line between questioning somebody's faith or religious practices and what could be cult or criminal activity. And it's hard to judge it from the outside especially if your spiritual vehicle isn't running right. Police and prosecutors have to be very careful. It would be easier for them to put this guy in jail on some money issue ... then some of the stuff that's been implicated."

"Just implicated?"

"I want to meet this man - this Pastor Thompson guy. Trust me here, it's as though Satan put on a cassock and he's got people afraid to even utter his name. That's what's going to make my job even harder, convincing them that they don't need to just tell me, they may need to tell a jury"

"So maybe that's why she's so evasive. She did say he might come looking for her."

"Now that's the really freaky thing. From the little information, I do have, he never went looking for any-body. They just wandered on back home. Prodigal sheep going in for the slaughter."

"Damn."

"Is that your favorite cuss word?"

"No, but it's about the only one I'm still repenting for. Sheep to slaughter, huh?"

"A word of advice ... Be careful. I've been looking into this stuff for about a month now; I'm determined to do something. So, if this young lady wants her sister and you don't want the job, I'll go get her."

"Why is this such a big deal for you? I mean, you're not a member of this church, and you haven't indicated that somebody you know is. What's the story?"

As Warren began speaking I did my best to under-stand what would set him off about this Pastor Thomp-son. For me, it was the continuing thought of what Anthony said, if you know something is wrong in the kingdom and you do nothing - then what? And now, it was about knowing what the man I'd been married to for five years had to do with this church and how did he know enough to feed an investigator some key informa-tion. And why did he come to Warren a month ago, when this is something he and I have only been at odds about for a week or two.

"One of the young men that ended up talking to investigators at the children and family services office has a permanent bruise on his back so prominent that even in the summer he wears a sweater or jacket so you can't see the imprint through his shirt."

"Jesus ... what ...how?"

"This guy is young, just married to a woman, a girl really, that the pastor chose. So now that he's got this wife, and he's working with the musicians, he's considered a leader. Pastor Thompson one night apparently set up a little live performance for his self-enjoyment. Apparently, he pairs young girls up with each other, telling them that they are prayer partners. Anyway, this guy walks in as Pastor Thompson has these two girls – the oldest of which is 15 - "praying for each other". In some sick kind of way, he's using Biblical scriptures to calm one girl who's totally freaking out."

"All of this happened in Miami?"

"No, this episode took place in a house behind a well-known chicken restaurant the church owned in Trenton, New Jersey- called, Chicken Delicious. This is how the guy relayed the story to me. I can read it just the way he wrote it, good writer too; or I can summarize it. It's like something from a movie. You sure you wanna hear this?"

"Yes, I do – please go ahead – read it to me, I'll take notes."

"Here's my – well here's this guy's story...." As Warren began the story I began scribbling notes trying to keep up with him, I struggled to visualize everything he would relay. I needed to know if the scenes in his script resembled mine.

"He was watching from some secret closet next to this room. Mahira and Yeshay were obviously uncomfortable in performing the tasks assigned them. They fumbled and groped unnaturally at each other, unsure of their moves, their thoughts, their lives. Yeshay's small, delicate hand faded into the folds of Pastor Thompson's sturdy and large hand, as he led her shaking fingers to Mahira's breasts. Mahira trembled at her touch and tears trickled down her face. Her breath heavy and labored could be seen in her chest and shoulders. Her apprehension seemed to anger Pastor Thompson. Yet, he gently wiped tears away from her face as he pulled her onto his lap. Yeshay, almost hypnotically knelt in a prayer position next to Pastor Thompson's feet.

"Mahira, my angel, there is nothing for you to be afraid of. Do you remember the story in second Samuel? Tamar laid with her brother Amnon. Her other brother Absalom told her 'hold now thy peace, my sister: he is thy brother; regard not this thing.' Do you know why Amnon laid with his sister? Because he loved her so much that he became sick trying to figure out how he could show her his love. Do you know what it is to lay with someone Mahira?"

"No Pastor, I don't." The tears covered her small neck decorated with a simple brown leather strap with a cowry shell in the center. She fought to hold back the tears.

"Of course, you don't. And that is why Yeshay and I are here to help you learn. Yeshay has been a sister to you since you were a baby. Don't you love her?"

Mahira nodded innocently.

"Then repent for your disrespect and disobedience and embrace your sister."

Mahira knelt in front of Yeshay, uttering a quick and sincere prayer. With tears still washing away her innocence, she embraced Yeshay. As the two girls tumbled to the floor and Pastor Thompson again guided Yeshay's hands about Mahira's body resting one in the folds of her garden. This guy decides he's seen enough and he goes busting through the bedroom door. Mupali's unwelcomed presence immediately angered, (enraged is the word he actually used) Pastor Thompson, who grabbed the young man by the neck throwing him against a wall.

"What are you doing here? You are not supposed to be here?"

"Pastor, please, please. Mahira's mother is looking for her. Please let me go Pastor."

Pastor Thompson loosened his grip, the two girls now more upset and more confused ran about the room gathering their clothes, but dared not dress before Pastor Thompson gave a nod of acknowledgment.

"Our sessions together Mahira and Yeshay are just like a time of fasting, you speak of it to no one, you just do it and know that the Lord will honor you for it. Do you understand me?"

The girls nodded and scrambled out of the room quickly. Mupali attempted to leave with the two young girls but was stopped short.

"You will never speak a word of this. The Bible says those the Lord loves he chastises. YOU HEAR ME BOY... this guy says Thompson started acting weird, says he closed his eyes as though he was listening to something or someone, then he says... Yes, Lord. You, boy, you have shown dishonor to my private room. Leave me alone."

I kept jotting down all this new information. My mind was racing with a multitude of questions and even more random prayers for every victim that Warren spoke of. Why are these kids not saying anything to their parents? What keeps the parents from confronting this guy? What Bible is he teaching from and is anyone reading and seeking understanding from God directly? How, in this day and age, is this kind of thing happening in the kingdom and no one knows? What happens in the minds and spirits of these little girls taught to molest each other and taught to allow themselves to be raped by a man old enough to be their father or grandfather?

"So anyway, this guy, whose name in case I was going too fast is Mupali; thinks he's going to be ex-communicated for a time or something like that. That however ain't quite how it worked out."

"This part doesn't sound like it's going to be too friendly."

"Not at all! If you don't want to...."

"Oh no, please go ahead. I need to know what happened."

"Mupali says these big six five and six four brothers came for him. He says it did not feel as though they had come to invite him to a time a fellowship. Brothers James and Johnny Williams were two of the original members and part of only a handful who were not forced to change their names. They were the head deacons as it were. Nobody really knows why Thompson and some of the original ones could keep their real names. My guess is they had already created some scams using their own personal information to get disability or some other kind of government assistance to have a consistent supply of money flowing in to finance church operations.

"But let me," Warren said, "keep on with the Mupali tale. Snatched from his wife, the young man who had witnessed the near premature awakening of two young girls was whisked to the airport and flown to the church's establishment in Ohio. Pastor Thompson had been preaching often about this new land and how the church would build a glorious kingdom there. The land was in southeast Ohio miles from any nearby cities, so he said and was plush with acres of green grass and trees and fertile ground for planting. It was, he said, a land of peace, and the church would make it a sanctified place of praise.

Unsure of what faced him and unable to run away since he had never been outside of the church's confines, Mupali willingly followed the two men to a waiting car. The drive through the city from the airport and to the far side of the church's farming area in Ohio seemed to take forever – but he says from the clock in the car it was about an hour. Mupali could see nothing but trees, there was nothing else distinguishable - no billboards, no houses that you could see from the road. He said he could tell from the sound of the car's tires that they were on a dirt road and there were several roadways that seemed to lead to one main highway.

The two deacons and the man that picked them up stayed quiet, no music came from the radio, instead it was an audio tape of one Pastor Thompson's favorite teachings,

"Walking in Your Calling". Mupali feared that his accidentally stumbling on the scene in New Jersey threatened his
calling. In his heart, he knew he would no longer be able
to play with the musicians; and he feared the wife he had
only known for two weeks before he married her would be
stripped away from him.

They came up on a rustic barn with what appeared
to be new metal doors. A striking contrast to what was
billed as a home of serenity – don't you think? On the
right of the barn is a big white house, with a huge porch
that covered the front and part of the left side of the
house. There were three or four big trucks parked in
front of the house and some boxes sat on the porch.
On the left of the barn was a smaller barn with wooden
doors closed with a huge chain and three or four dead
bolt locks. There was a lot of land. Miles and miles of
trees and grass.

Anyway, Mupali says his heart began to race franti-
cally, but he did not speak. When the back door of the car
was pulled open he sat still, not wanting to move, feeling
suddenly like moving would mean his death. As they
pulled him from the car the three men reminded Mupali
of the same Biblical teaching that Pastor Thompson did,
"whom the Lord loves, he does chastise."

Now Mupali's scared out of his mind so he starts ram-
bling. Where is Pastor Thompson? I need to speak with
the Pastor, to apologize.

'Pastor knows that you are sorry, still you have to be
chastised. It is a mandate of the Lord and it is up to us as
the church to fulfill his mandates.' That's what the guys
tell him.

Twelve men were standing in this barn that was doubling for an office. He knew that because he saw a desk and some chairs, file cabinets, bunch of junk like that. These men to Mupali looked like huge trees, he was like the blind man that had just been granted sight. What he was seeing though was not miraculous. You've got twelve deacons all stern faced wearing plastic overalls which means some serious shi... stuff is about to happen. Anyhow, they are all lined up in the middle of this barn side by side, face to face, six on one side, six on the other. None of them look at him. Says their faces didn't even move. He tried the religious small talk, blessing them in greeting, asking about families - all that kind of foolishness. They just stood there like old oak trees too rooted to be cut down.

With their hands folded behind their backs, one of the men led them into a prayer that seemed to have been designed just for Mupali. Something about touching the anointed, betraying the covenant, bringing dishonor to the prophet. The words he said sent shivers through him and in a moment, in a second, he says he believed that God had left him and instead sent His wrath upon him. Before the final Amen was muttered, Mupali felt something swift and sharp slice across his back. He turned to face the source of the pain that resonated through him, as he did; there was yet another crash this time catching his shoulder and the side of his face.

The crashing went on for several moments stinging every inch of his five eleven, 190-pound frame, until he "crashed" to the floor. Still the beatings continued. Mupali says he felt a strong and urgent chill cut along his spine.

Though there was nothing he could do, he reacted to the coolness on his back and tried to cover himself. Touching his back lightly, he felt the blood all over him and then he slipped into unconsciousness.

Ms. Adams, they beat this boy so bad, they literally put a gash ten inches long, three inches deep and three inches wide in his back. Then they had some mother stitch him up."

"What happened to him after that?"

"Thompson gave his wife to someone else in New Jersey and he was left in Ohio. The church here and in Jersey was told he was ex-communicated for a time for striking the pastor."

"Needless to say, nobody wanted anything to do with him."

"Hell no! About six weeks later the Ohio church gets a couple of frantic phone calls and all the deacons pulled up heading to Jersey. About three to four days later they come back with a big group of young people, including the two girls Mupali had seen doing the foreplay thing. Mupali never said anything else about anything. As far as they were concerned, the Lord made him quiet; shut up his mouth for good. I can tell you this; he put those kids out there for one major orgy training ground. I got stories from farmers peeping through trees watching stuff. Police couldn't do anything, nobody could identify the kids and so there was no proof that any of the people involved in the sexcapades were part of First Alliance. I guess they figured who would know or see in the woods of Ohio?"

"Where were their parents? But Cathy did tell me, it was always a privilege to travel with or go to Pastor's house; so, it stands to reason the parents were cool about it."

"Probably. But didn't these kids start acting differently – wouldn't your kid be terrified if some man had him doing something he didn't want to? They had to know something."

"No maybe not. I was asking myself the same thing while you were talking. But, think about it. I'm 12, 15, all I have ever known is this church, this pastor – my momma and daddy are in this church, they trust him, they listen to him. If I do not understand how God works aside from what this guy is telling me, then my level of intimidation is already high. But, I love him so much, so very much … he's my pastor, he baptized me, he christened me, I can go to his house whenever I want to. I'm scared yeah, but I've always been cool about it because my Pastor pays so much attention to me. Now, you and I might call it fear. Except it's not fear for these kids, its reverence and respect, and the level of that reverence and respect is higher than what they have for their own parents."

"Can that really be possible? "

"You don't go to church, do you?"

"Is this going to be an altar call?"

"All right, no, but that's the way it is in the church. You have situations like that all the time. Parents can't do anything with a kid, but they get around the pastor and it's a totally different attitude. They suddenly don't suck their teeth, and they don't dare cuss like they were just doing outside and they're not running around pinching each other's stuff. Cause, I'm in front of pastor."

"I'm in front of God."

"Exactly. It happens in some marriages too. That's why I think it's so hard for black men in church. You always talking about the pastor this and the pastor that, you got more love and paying more attention to the pastor then you are to your husband. If the pastor says you be in church every night for the two-week conference; but your husband says you need to be home, you go to church. Then you tell yourself and people that the devil is disrupting your marriage.

"Misguided loyalty."

"Exactly. Then let's look at this way. If what you're telling me about Mupali is true, and if what Cathy told me is true, then the parents are just as scared. But you believe that you are living according to God, because this is what this man is teaching you and how dare you go against God – how dare you go against his messenger. The Bible tells us that the Word will come through the prophet, or in contemporary times, the preacher. I bet you there is one main thing he teaches, and he probably works it into every sermon..."

"And that would be..."

"Touch not my anointed. Touch not my anointed. If I'm going to twist stuff around, you better believe, the first thing I'm going to do is make you terrified to do or say anything against me. From what I've found in research and in personal stories, it gets so real in cult situations that even if God reveals the evil to you, you are more afraid of the preacher than of the wrath of God. And if you do not, I mean never, allow me to ever spend any time alone – any time with God; I'm bound to trust you more."

"When do you think for yourself though?"

"Come on now, that's not allowed. I'm going to get you involved in twelve ministries. I'm going to appoint you and dis-appoint you at will. I'm going to give you a special name, move you away from everybody, keep you paired up or grouped up and keep you sinning, so that I can always remind you that you are not worthy of God. You are a sinner, look what you did before God. I discourage you from talking to God by telling you, He does not speak to you directly, He speaks to you only through the prophet."

"So then aren't all preachers tying people up in bondage?"

"Not all of them, just those that instill that kind of behavior. It's not as serious in the implementation of the teaching, but the message is still the same. Touch not my anointed. Don't question the anointed; just do what the anointed says."

"And what about you? Do you touch "the anointed"?"

"I may not have a choice. Listen you mind if I call you again?" I took one more look at the various pads and boards that painted the First Alliance picture around Warren's office. The details in the painting were intricate and frightening. "You're going to get her, aren't you?" He helped me gather my things and handed me copies of files.

"I may not have a choice."

"You keep saying that. This can get really deep and you cannot approach or question this guy alone. I don't care what's going on in your head, trust me this man is dangerous at worst – insane in the least. Remember this – Satan in a cassock."

"You sound like my husband. Why does either one of us care? It's not my family or yours, not my friends or yours. Why does either one of us care?"

"Because if he pulled this on somebody's grand-mother, daughter, son, wife – he could very well get my family or yours. And because, hell, every once in a while, you get the chance to do something just because you see a chance to. Personally, I never learned not to take those chances and I don't think you have either. By the way Mrs. Houston..."

"Adams."

"I know you're Anthony's wife. He told me you would call me. He also said that he knows you're going to that conference and that I'm to go with you to make sure you don't get carried away."

"Why did Anthony come to you?"

"I can't tell you that."

"What does he know?"

"I can't tell you that either. I can't break a client's con-fidence and I certainly cannot tell a wife, things she needs to hear from her husband."

"So, what you're telling me is Anthony may have some first hand, actually involved in knowledge of this First Alliance situation?"

"No, I'm not telling you that. I'm simply saying a man knows his woman and knows how to tell her what's going on with him. I'd be less of a man if I interfered with that."

"Well, can you at least te...."

"I will tell you this; he and I both know Cathy English is not telling you the truth. Personally, I think Thompson wants your husband and what better way to get him, than to a have a lost lamb befriend the perpetual Good Samaritan. What time you going to the conference?" I shrugged my shoulders not really interested in the conference any more.

"Why does Thompson want my husband?"

"I really think you need to ask him that. It's just what I get at the end of the maze building in my little First Alliance command center. I could very well be wrong."

By the time, I reached the elevator in Warren's building I was dialing Anthony's cell number. No answer. Looking at my watch I realized that his flight was probably just taking off. Hearing his voice inviting me to leave a message both angered me and broke me down. "Oh, my God, what is going on and why does Anthony not want to talk to me about this?" I pressed the call end button as the beep on the other end signified that my voice message could begin.

Stepping into the elevator, I smiled at the very attractive young man that was also taking the ride down. His left dimple was a nice accompaniment to the dazzling diamond earrings in both ears. It was rare that a young brother in a full business suit crossed my path. I had seen his suit recently in a magazine, it was from the new Sean John business and evening collection and he wore it well. Black with a dark blue tie with speckles of gold and black shoes. I'm sure he thought the gasp of breath was a sign of my pleasure in what I saw; it instead was my effort to keep from screaming. In such a contemporary suit, the old-school footwear was out of place. These shoes were not only like the ones in my dream; they were like a pair Anthony kept in the far corners of his side of the closet. He never wears them and while he cleans out the closet often and donates things to different charities – those shoes stay there. They stay there.

Talk to Me
In Hidden Messages

Chapter Nine

Charlotte, North Carolina's airport was busier than I had seen it in quite a while. Most of the flights, I assumed, must be connecting ones during the middle of the day and it was just my luck to land right in the middle of the bustling to get to the next gate and the next flight. I pulled the cell phone from my carryon bag and checked for messages. Crystal's number, no message. By now, I knew she was good and pissed off and probably disturbed and confused. I should have told her before I left instead of taking time to hold her after breakfast reminiscing on the date we had that ended with both of us getting drenched in the rain because she locked the keys in the car. While tender moments are significant and necessary in every loving relationship, I knew that it was just an avoidance tactic for me. Crystal being told the truth - that I knew exactly why the nightmares consumed her and knew what they showed her, was not something I was prepared to face. I was being a punk.

There was a message from Warren Levy. I met Warren a few years ago, through a friend's recommendation.

When a former associate thought it necessary to embezzle money from the company we founded together, I thought it necessary to find my money and get it back. Warren helped me do that. When I started getting clues in my spirit that William Thompson was about to act the fool, I hired Warren to find out where he was before he found me. I had to be smart about this. I needed to make sure he went down for more than tax evasion or fraud. Thompson needed to be disrobed and de-flocked or he would continue to pervert the kingdom of God and numerous underage girls.

I had enough information and knew where enough former and truly delivered members were to feed Warren. What I did not know, Warren had done an amazing job of finding out. Leaving First Alliance was painless and seamless for me. There was no major escape, no grand exit - I simply walked away with a photo of Fujana in my hand. The photo of her erotically detailed; it was of her in bed and high in the saddle - traces of chocolate sauce and whipped cream adorning her body, with James Taylor-Thompson; a very prominent pastor in Atlanta. More importantly he was, and probably still is, a man that Pastor Thompson despised because Taylor-Thompson's church was larger and far more prosperous than anything he had built. They apparently had attended seminary together and what many thought initially was a friendly rivalry, became attempts to destroy each other personally and in the ministry. The other photo which was merely a change in position during their afternoon together, I left beneath Fujana's hotel door with a note that one of the maids in the hotel wrote for me, all it said was "don't come looking for him". How she explained what happened to Pastor, I don't know and I don't care. I moved to Pasadena for a while, then to Houston and finally back to the northeast. By then I was 22-23 and I had learned enough of the street game on my trips with Fujana to get by and to start over.

In finding myself, my mother - the one who raised me, provided me with a lot of insight. The mothers in the church all had private phones in their homes so that the deacons could call on them during or after a time of chastisement; because of that I could and did call her from time to time. She sent me letters that connected some pieces I never knew were disjointed. She loved me, but she did not birth me, the woman who was so blessed died in labor. The young woman that I ran around with and called my sister, because that's what we did in the church, was in fact my sister and if I ever wanted to know what my mother looked like all I needed to do was look at her. My mother then, like my sister, was beauty dipped in glory and coated with butterscotch.

When I look at Crystal that is what I see. Beauty dipped in glory and coated with caramel. As God lives and reigns in heaven I don't want to lose that woman. How do I even begin to tell her that the man she met and married was literally born three times? Once to a mother who never held me and never heard her son's first cry. Once to my own self as a new man in and of himself, new name, new identity, new life. Once and most importantly, born again in Christ. Warren picked up the phone on the second ring.

"Warren Levy here, how can I help you?"

"Yo man, it's Houston. I take it you met Crys."

"That I did. You might as well know she's more than a little bothered with you, boy. And probably with me for not telling her what I know about you and this shit."

"Just watch her man. I'm going to reschedule my last meeting on this round of deals and try to get back there. I'm sure you can tell she's got a mind of her own..."

"I'll watch her man. You need to know that Thompson is expected to lead the conference in Miami next week. Tell me the truth man, you know what he wants don't you?"

"Yeah, I do, but I'll tear up heaven, hell and earth to keep him from getting it."

"It's you - isn't it man? He wants you - right?"

"You been watching too many Perry Mason or Matlock reruns again boy. I'll holler at you later."

"Yo man."

"Wassup."

"You could have told me she was fine enough for me to have check myself."

"Boy, don't make me hurt you. Just remember all of that is mine and I don't share."

Walking to the street exit of the airport I found myself struggling far too hard to decide if I would rent a car or just take a taxi to the hotel. Really it should have been a no-brainer, I was staying in the hotel where the meeting was taking place. One shot, close the contract, make the money, chill a minute and get back to Miami before my wife and my whole world disappear.

Before I flagged down a taxi, I found a quiet spot behind a column and called home. I didn't even hear the phone ring, but I clearly heard the distress in what normally is a very seductive, teasing voice when I called home.

"Why is a man that I don't know, more aware of what's going with my husband than I am?"

"Crystal, I've been trying to tell you that there are..."

"Don't talk to me in hidden messages. Anthony tell me now what is with you and this First Alliance mess?"

"Baby listen, I'm standing in front of the airport in North Carolina, let me get to the hotel so we can talk and I'll..."

"No. No. No. No. No. No. No. No. No. Tell me now..."

"Crys, twenty minutes girl and everything I know...."

Click. This time I was not in control of where the conversation went. There was nothing I was going to say to her that she would accept at this point except everything I had not said. I waved a cab down and stared out the window to nothing as the driver wove his way through traffic to the hotel. I opened the hotel room door and stared at the phone as I unloaded my luggage, laptop and briefcase onto the bed. Retrieving the receiver, I called home, hoping this call would be the first step to all of this being over.

I sat in the middle of the bed surrounded by newspaper clippings, note pads and Bibles. This scene over the last few weeks had begun to play itself out far too often in my house. This time though I was looking for an Anthony connection. I have never heard anyone call him anything besides Anthony, so I would not have known about any made up African sounding name. It had been two days since I'd met Warren Levy. It had been two days since I'd talked to Anthony. Numbers from hotel rooms, his cell number would flash on the caller ID and I would not answer. I did not want to hear any more delays - I wanted to know what he had gotten us into and why he kept trying to warn me away from something that was already evident.

Warren had filled my head with enough stories to make me dig deeper into First Born, Yahweh and other groups. Why is it you never hear about black cults the way you heard about the Branch Davidians and others? Pondering where I would find a story in all of this, and still trying to deny the thoughts of Anthony being a part of all this, I set about the business of trying to connect common threads when a story on the evening news pulled my attention.

"Days after the world learned of the Movement for the Restoration of the Ten Commandments of God, author- ities in Uganda pulled 80 more bodies from the reddish earth at a fourth compound connected to the Christian doomsday sect. This today as investigators in the African community questioned a former local official about the cult. Prisoners from a local jail exhumed the grave in Rush- ojwa, in southwestern Uganda. About 724 bodies have been found so far in four cult compounds. A fifth property has yet to be excavated. The recent recoveries bring the death toll to more than the infamous Jim Jones tragedy in Guyana a little more than 20 years ago. Most of the bod- ies found were those of women and girls. A woman who

lives near the cluster of four tin roof buildings with practically nothing inside them, said many have worried about what was happening there. Authorities have launched an international manhunt for the two main leaders of the movement -- Cledonia Mwerinde, a former prostitute – believed to be the group's founder and major leader; and Joseph Kibwetere, an excommunicated Roman Catholic. The pair, acting allegedly on conversations with and signs from the Virgin Mary, had predicted that the world would end Dec. 31, 1999 and therefore ordered members to turn over all their worldly possessions including money. When the reported doomsday did not come to pass, authorities believe cult members demanded the return of the possessions. The uprising, according to authorities probably led to the strangling, poisoning and burning of hundreds. The death toll is expected to rise once the fifth property is excavated. Police in Uganda have been unable to identify the dead. Still to come ... the owner of the Florida Marlins has some strong opposition to the building of a new stadium, that plus weather and sports next..."

The news sent chills through me, another mass killing under the guise of a church affiliation. This was the group that I had pulled up the clip on, but I didn't get a chance to watch it. Now this. Who were the members of the Movement for the Restoration of the Ten Commandments of God? I began another frantic Internet search – as far-fetched as it seemed could there be a connection between the Movement and Thompson's church. One of the headlines nearly floored me, it was almost the exact same description Levy had used in describing Thompson – but this one was much more direct – "A Devil in Angel's Robes".

The reporter's description was of Cledonia Mwerinde. Mwerinde, a beautiful woman with intriguing dark eyes, reportedly developed her spiritual richness after seeing an apparition of the Virgin Mary in a southwestern Ugandan cave, near the village of Nga-kishenyi. Her former lover told investigators it was all a scam she cooked up after their business went bankrupt. Prior to that she sold banana beer and liquor and occasionally her body. Her 12 'apostles' were family members.

All the patterns were the same; she rose to power quickly, operated with an iron fist, and restricted the movement and contact of church members with outsiders, under the pre-tense of it being part of heavenly visions. She even denied soap and basic hygiene items to members and ordered them to turn over all their possessions as the end of the world drew near.

The Mwerinde story was especially disturbing because it seemed in all the uncovering of bodies and the testimonies of those that had some knowledge of the church, Mwerinde, though a woman, deliberately and cruelly forced women and children to suffer. I shut down the computer and began to gather the papers that still lay scattered about the bed. As I did the small clipping about the conference fell, landing at my feet. Looking at the dates again, I thought it best to just ignore the whole thing and not go to the conference to avoid Ant's questioning and ranting and at this point to avoid my attempting to question him again.

I don't ever remember a time in our dating or since we've been married that we've gone half a day let alone two days without talking to each other when either of us is on the road. I did not like not talking to him. But I did not like feeling like he was lying to me or deliberately holding something back from me. Even with all of that in my heart, I found myself picking up the phone and calling Maggie.

"Hey girl – what's going on?" I pulled lettuce, tomatoes, cucumbers and Cajun seasoned chicken breast strips from the frig, preparing to make myself a healthy and lite meal.

"Nothing much, doing my hair, that's the highlight of my life on a Friday night. I guess that's what becomes of a single woman when all her girlfriends get married."

Maggie always complained about her marital status versus the status of her closest friends. Why I could never figure out. Maggie was a workaholic, but she was a playaholic too. Which meant, if she worked a double shift then decided to take off three days and spend time in Bermuda, she did that. She is a party girl and it didn't matter if the party was the Essence Festival in July, or the Goombay Festival in June, or Mardi Gras in the spring - she was going to be there. That was a freedom you didn't necessarily enjoy with marriage. Did I miss rolling like that? Sometimes, but not often. The simple fact of the matter is I'm happy in marriage like Maggie is happy in the single life; because Maggie and I have two very different needs. I need to be secure in my man's arms and heart. Maggie needs to be secure in knowing the man she's with knows he's not welcome to see the sunrise next to her.

"There is hope for you yet. Listen; want to take a field trip with me tomorrow? I'm investigating something for a possible story."

"What are you investigating?"

"A possible cult. Wait..."

"You want me to go to a cult meeting? Weren't the voodoo shops in New Orleans enough? Wasn't the crying episode at the factory on Jekyll Island and you telling me someone is under there talking to you enough? What is it with you? Do you need to have some kind of exorcism or something?"

"You are so dramatic and overdone sometimes girl. Here's the nutshell version. Those nightmares I've been having; I think may be about this cult that a girl at church was a member of. She approached me about helping her get her sister, who is still in the cult out. Don't worry, I didn't agree to that – but I know the nightmares and this church are connected; and I want to know why."

"And what did Anthony say?"

"He told me to stay away from them until he gets back in town."

"And so, we would be going, knowing it's going to piss him off because..."

"Because it's a prime opportunity. Look I met this investigator guy, Warren, seems this church/cult is under investigation for fraud or racketeering – but he's uncovered some wild stuff. I'll ask him to go with us. I just gotta know Maggie, I gotta know."

"And - what are we looking for?"

"I don't know. But I'll know when I feel it."

"That is scary. I'll go with you, but Crys – don't let your inability to control your imagination get us into trouble. All right?"

"I'll try not to. I'll call Warren now. Listen, we should probably try to fit in as much as possible, so be real conservative okay. Like a very traditional Pentecostal church, long skirts that kind of thing. Cool?"

"Awrighty then. I don't know how you get me into this stuff."

"Because you don't have a life."

"Reminding me of that is not a good thing."

"What are you doing to your hair now? You just put braids in last week."

I munched on my salad as Maggie recounted how she looked in the mirror that morning and realized the couple of gray strands that she originally thought were cute, had bombarded her entire scalp. Color number 654 she said was her defense in the battle to reclaim the territory.

Warren's phone rang several times before he finally picked up. He was somewhat surprised to hear from me. "Well Mrs. Houston, I have to tell you I figured your husband had talked you out of this story – I haven't heard from you."

"He's out of town; you know that I'm sure. Are you going to that First Alliance Holiness conference this weekend?"

"I was going to check it out. Why? Please don't tell me you're still thinking about going especially after everything I told you."

"I want to see what this church is all about. My husband's been to see you about this. Cathy English nearly

peed her pants when he asked if he knows her. He's
warned me about different articles before, but this time
he's scared. I am now fully aware that there is something too close to my home about this whole thing. And
I gotta figure out what it is. My girl Maggie is going to
go with me, but I promised her we'd take you. And you
obviously already promised Anthony, that you'd look
out for me."

"He did say you are the epitome of stubborn. Listen,
this could be dangerous. We need to plan our moves carefully. What time is it?"

"A little after seven."

"You mind coming here; I'm waiting for a fax from
another one of Thompson's former members."

"Did you see the news tonight?"

"Yeah, you talking about the Ten Commandments
Movement."

"They called her a devil in an angel's robes, that's the
same thing you said about Thompson. You think there's
a supernatural message there. That you and this reporter
would have the same image of this kind of evil."

"Maybe the reporter is black."

"And so."

"And so, then he would have a black grandmother
who might have told him the same thing mine told me.
You can't let everybody tell you 'bout Jesus, you gotta
know Him for yourself."

"Give me about an hour, my husband should be
checking in in just a little while and I have to assure
him I'm okay. This is the first time he's been gone since

I started having those nightmares and well we haven't talked since I left your office the other day."

"Yeah, I know. He's had me come past the house several times to make sure you were there. What nightmares?"

"I'll tell you about it when I see you. Listen, have you found out anything else on this guy?"

"Yeah, but nothing that can't wait. I'll see you in a while."

Tasting the evil in this mess

Chapter Ten

Hanging up the phone, I stacked separate piles of papers into manila file folders and stuffed them into my portfolio. I then flipped through my closet to see what would be appropriate to wear to the conference and decided on a dark blue suit I hadn't worn since Anthony's aunt's funeral. Pulling a t-shirt and a pair of jeans from the closet, the ringing phone startled me and I picked it up abruptly.

"Hey beautiful, how you doing? You miss me yet?"

"About as much as you're missing me. When you coming back?"

"Sunday I promise. No more delays. You deserve more than my putting you off. You're not sleeping, are you?"

"I'm okay – I take cat naps. I'm afraid to sleep here without you."

"You should have come with me. I told you that."

"No. You shouldn't be lugging your wife around to multi-thousand-dollar business deals; I'll be fine, until you get back. If push comes to shove, I'll spend the night at Maggie's."

"Maggie left a message on my cell."

"I could kill her."

"It's comforting to know that I'm not the only one who knows you're walking into something dangerous. What did Warren tell you?"

"He's going to the conference too, so he's going to look out for me and Maggie."

"He won't have to."

"Anthony ..."

"Anthony hell, I told you to stay away from those people and I mean it. I know I told him to look out for you – because I knew you would go over there. Crystal, you don't know what you're up against, but I do. For once – listen to me woman – for once. Crys – are you there? Crystal!"

"I'm here. Anthony..."

"Tell me you won't go. Crystal I'm talking to you. Oh, okay. Fine. Then just hang up the phone."

And he did. What was going on? In the years we've been together, Anthony has never been so uptight about me getting involved in investigative pieces. Not the piece on the drug boys, not the piece on notorious street gangs that won me the Associated Press Award, not the piece on domestic violence at its worst – that ended up with me and one victim being held hostage by a deranged lover. What was so disturbing about this potential story for Anthony? Why, even knowing it was causing him so much pain, was I determined to walk head first into hell fire? And again, came the question, what does Anthony know about First Born Alliance and why am I now afraid that my husband is involved in all of this?

With Anthony's demand for me to stay away or hang up the phone still ringing in my ear, I climbed into the truck Anthony left in the drive way with a beautiful purple bow and a note that read, "at some point you have to trade every vehicle in. You'll get used to this truck just like you did the first one. I love you darling. Be careful." Lord I love that man. What is he hiding from me?

I arrived at Warren's office a little past eight o'clock. I passed the pizza man in the corridor and realized that I hadn't eaten dinner. As I entered the office Warren extended his hand and a chicken wing, much to my pleasure.

"What's wrong? You've been crying."

"Had an argument with Anthony."

"About the conference?"

"Don't risk your marriage for a story. I'm going, I can find out as much as possible. How'd he know you were going to go after all?"

"My best friend Maggie called him, out of concern I guess. He was just pissed. I never heard that kind of emotion in his voice."

"Fear... Mrs. Houston...."

"Crystal."

"Crystal – these people are dangerous. And don't think for a minute your husband hasn't looked at every note, every piece of paper you've pulled off the Internet. And without betraying his confidence, let me say this – don't think he's not fully aware of this particular evil. I never asked him, but I could tell, he's a church going man, right?"

"Of course."

"Well don't think he's not concerned that you're not tasting the evil in this mess. You're moving ahead of him, and he's not here to put his hands on you. Hell, don't be surprised if he gets a plane back here tonight. Trust me, Crystal – a man can recognize trouble – and this Rev. Thompson is trouble. Another case, Nujara – she just had one name – Nujara. No one knew what happened to her. She is the daughter of the man that used to be Thompson's right hand man in Ohio. He went crazy and Thompson had him committed. Turns out he may have had help going crazy. Nujara was 14 when she began to be prepared for ministry to the Pastor. Much like pre-wedding rites in Africa and Haiti the women would prepare all kinds of oil and herbs and rub it on your body while the fragrances of incense filled your nostrils. Then they would pass a communal cup of grape juice and each woman would give you a bit of wisdom as the cup was passed on."

"So, at 14 they were preparing her to sleep with the Pastor?"

"Oh yeah. He apparently didn't like them over 21 or so."

"How nice? His wife was for what?"

"Respectable show in the community. Training up the young women. Number trois in the ménage. Very well taken care of. I saw that movie, was it Women of Brewster's Place, where the preacher would go over to one girl's apartment for a little special healing service. Sunday afternoon he's getting his fried chicken and a little more than finger licking too. Everybody knows but nobody says anything. And remember that old movie, they show on Black Starz all the time, Sister, Sister when Diahann

Carroll was the epitome of a church going woman, condemning everybody and all the while she was sleeping
with the married preacher; until he slept with her sister. I
guess what I'm saying is it obviously ain't that unusual in
our churches. I know you a church lady and all and saw is
my grandma and mama; but if I ever wanted to get free -
um, well you know - on call, I'd become a preacher. Don't
tell my grandma I said that."

"You really think it's that rampant?"

"People say good fiction is always based on the
truth, so if you got different movies in different times
popping up with the preacher getting his thing handled
by women around him no questions asked – that says
there's some truth. You don't think that happens in your
church?"

"Let's just say – my prayer will be that every woman
understands who she is first in God and secondly in herself and that respect to those two people is what you must
sleep with every night."

"That's deep. Anyway, where was I? Oh, the day finally
comes and Nujara is positioned for her time of nourishment with Thompson. She says they call it the bow
position, most of us just call it, excuse my French, doggie
style."

"He didn't want to look at her?"

"No, because you see Nujara is actually his daughter."

"What?"

"Her mother was forced much the way she was. But
she became pregnant, Thompson's wife convinced her to
marry Deacon Mushal Jabu. They slept together immediately. He thinks the kid is his."

"David and Bathsheba. What does that have to do with him going crazy?"

"David and Bathsheba?"

"Bible lesson. David sees woman sun bathing out his palace window, sexes her, she ends up pregnant, and David goes out of his way to pull a whole lot of strings to get her husband back from war to sleep with her so he'll think the kid is his. You said the deacon went crazy."

"Well turns out, Nujara knew the truth, her mother apparently told her because it was killing her inside and because she wanted out. When Thompson started, she yelled, 'Daddy please don't do this to me.' Thompson freaked out, and had the child hung up on a cross for two days and every time he thought about what she did, he'd cover her face and rape her. Her father came back from Akron, found his wife in the bathtub, with a matching pair of slit wrists. But she was alive long enough to tell him the truth and what Thompson had been doing to her and her daughter. He went out to the house, the private house, and sure enough he found Thompson raping his daughter and Mrs. Thompson helping him do it. Nujara said five men beat her father out the door. Five women, then beat her into unconsciousness."

"Then what?"

"Nujara says God stopped her breathing. When He did, they thought she was dead. The women carried her out into the woods about five miles away from the house and left her under a tree. The men were supposed to come back to dig her grave. She lay there until she couldn't hear them, and then ran."

"Where was she running to?"

"She says she just ran until she found a road, she went in the direction away from where the church was located. Two miles down the road, she wondered up on an old lady who took her in."

"So, she was right under their noses."

"Of course, it was probably the best place to be. This little old lady told her for days, they would have people watching the train station and the bus station, the airport. At the restaurant where they, everybody in the church, worked people would ask where she was and they just said she went back to school in Ohio."

"What did she do? And why didn't she or the lady call the police?

"She stayed with this woman until she was 18. You believe that shit, four years, and she's right under their nose and they don't know it. When she turned 18, she and the woman moved to Miami, to be closer to the lady's sister and so that Nujara could go to the University of Miami. She could never find out anything about her father and she heard them say her mother was dead, the day they left her in the woods. They never called the police, because it would have been the word of a 14-year-old runaway against a Pastor, who is well-respected in the surrounding community, although his church members don't come and go as they please."

"So how did you find her?"

"She and Mupali happened up on each other one day and have kept in touch. She and your husband are very close. He told her about what was going on and she called me. And I'm sure I shouldn't tell you this but you've met her – the older woman that is – you and your husband buried an aunt about two years ago, right?"

"Yes, we did. That was her?"

"One person did know where she and Nujara were. Anthony. She says he is the reason she never went back."

"What does that mean? And how does she feel about this conference tomorrow?"

"She's scared but she wants to take him out, so she's willing to help me do that. Said whatever she needs to do, she believes she's strong enough to handle it. Besides she says she owes to her mama."

"But he doesn't know she's here, right?"

"No, but Lashay does. And she says Lashay is unstable and dangerous."

"Who is Lashay?"

"Well, I'm not really sure, but I got a feeling it's your Ms. English. If not, Pastor Brighton's got two or maybe more of Thompson's former members running around his church."

"What? Cathy English is Lashay?"

"Only one way to find out."

"Can I use your phone?"

"Sure, be my guess."

"Warren, Nujara. I know her as Nisa Houston, right?"

His smile answered what his words could not.

Eli, Eli, Lama Sabachthani

Chapter Eleven

Anthony had left a message. The sound of his voice worried me. The message itself did more than worry me, it cautioned me.

"Crys it's me. I know you're not going to listen to me and I know you're going to some part of that conference tonight or this weekend; just please give me enough time to get back in town tomorrow morning. Just DO NOT go until I talk to you. There IS something you need to know. Just please wait for me."

The second message gave even more credence to the assertion that Cathy English might in fact be Lashay and that Lashay is definitely unstable.

"Ms. Houston, this is Cathy English. I've been thinking about our talk and maybe this isn't what the Lord wants. Maybe I should leave it alone. Pastor preached Sunday that sometimes you've got to get your own deliverance right. And I know he was talking about me. Did you tell him about our conversation, I hope you didn't, I mean if you did, maybe he could help us."

Confused by the tone of both calls, I fell onto the couch, pulling my legs up to my chest and cried. And there really was no reason for the tears. I was just frustrated and I didn't know what else to do. I didn't want to read any more about any of these crazy religions, I didn't want to fight with Anthony again, so I didn't call his hotel. I did want to tell Cathy English that a good psychiatrist is always an option, and I did want to tell Maggie I felt betrayed. I also wanted to go to sleep – I wanted to go and to stay asleep. And as the tears flowed harder, I had to admit that I wanted my husband. I wanted him to take care of all this craziness. I wanted him to tell me why he had this whole life I didn't know about.

"Father what is all of this about? Why is my Ant so mad at me? I'm not trying to get into anything; I'm not understanding any of this. Not the nightmares, not the cults, not this man raping and beating people in your name. I don't understand why no one has put this man away. And I don't understand how I ended up right in the middle of the intersection where everything collides."

Without even knowing it, I had fallen soundly asleep on the couch. When I again felt the warming of my body that preceded the dreams, I tried to wake up. I could feel myself looking for an entry way to an awakened state. But it was to no avail. Not even my falling from the couch to the floor woke me up. The nightmares began again.

Jesus hung on the cross and to His right, a soiled and shaking 14-year-old girl cries, and to His left, a battered and beaten young man cries and Jesus wept. At their feet, was Thompson condemning the actions that he said put them in this position. The crowd stood motionless, never taking their eyes off Thompson, never realizing the symbolism of Thompson condemning Jesus on the cross and crucifying his own sins. A woman burst through the crowd, her hands shivering. While blood dripped from her wrists she reached towards the young girl. Then there were the black leather shoes again and a large hand against her face forced her to the ground.

The ground swallowed her up and Adele Thompson looked in her husband's eyes and said, "What else can we do? This is too much now". And the hand that went with the black leather shoes hit her repeatedly, and the congregation stood motionless and Jesus and the children screamed, 'Eli, Eli, lama sabachthani! Eli, Eli, lama sabachthani! Eli, Eli, lama sabachthani! Eli, Eli, lama sabachthani! And I heard myself screaming – I have not! Don't you hear Him; he has not forsaken you.' Suddenly I felt someone's arms encircle my waist and as quickly as I was thrust into the nightmares, I found a peaceful place in my sleep.

The ringing phone urged me awake the next morning. Looking about the room I struggled to remember how I ended up on the floor and why I had fallen asleep in my clothes. As I glanced up at the clock, I realized I was running behind schedule and only had forty minutes to get dressed and downtown. I'd already decided that I would not call Maggie – that was an unnecessary conversation at this point. Rushing about the house, I could hear Anthony's message playing in my head, "just don't go until I get there. I have to tell you something." And for the first time since hearing the message, my mind went forward to the actual end of that same message, "and prayerfully when I tell you, you won't walk away from me."

Pondering why I hadn't paid any attention to that line before now, I found myself putting my shoes on the wrong feet – that was something I hadn't done since I was about three or was it the last time I got drunk at a sorority party. What would be so terrible about this man that I've slept next to and with for so long, that I would even think about walking away from him? The nightmares I told myself were not things I was familiar with, but what happened in the awake realm was something I needed to comprehend. When the nightmares belonged to Anthony, we would beg me to never let go of him. Maybe that was because the reality of the dreams was more than he could bear at the time. Stumbling through the massive articles and research that I'd pulled in the last few weeks, I wondered if Ant was one of these men convicted of killing someone for Yahweh Ben Yahweh – surely, my spirit comforted me – that is not it. My imagination had gone way out in left field.

I pushed the thought back in my mental left field folder, grabbed my keys and tore out of the driveway. I met Warren at the hotel about ten minutes later than we had planned. As I looked around the lobby of the Marriott Courtyard, I thought about how much livelier and classier it looked now than it did when it was a Holiday Inn or was it Howard Johnson's. I remembered getting a media invite to tour the remodeled hotel with its completely new furnished rooms and redesigned meeting rooms and it did look good. I guess there was really something in gutting and starting all over.

From the title of the sessions going on as part of this church retreat, it was obvious that they were likewise looking to do some starting over, but just how much of the old practices had been gutted remained to be seen. Warren and I peeked in on a couple of sessions that seemed normal for church conferences – the one on the responsibilities of church leadership additionally served as the general session. We decided to sit in on that one. Out of nowhere, my heart started racing as though I was right in the middle of one of those high-speed carnival rides that toss you to and fro. My breaths quickened and I felt myself trembling.

"Crystal, you okay? You really don't look too good. Maybe we should go. I promised your husband I'd watch out for you."

"No, no, Warren. I'm fine. It's just that man."

"What man? The one preaching?"

"Yes, it's him. The one from the newspaper clippings. That's him, isn't it?"

"Yep. That's old Pastor William Thompson in the flesh. You can almost see how he can intimidate the life out of people."

Thompson, as I stared at him did in fact look intimidating. He stood there in this light that made him appear easily eight feet tall, the sound system balanced just right so that the tenor quality of his voice echoed deep inside of you. You literally felt each of his words stir in the pit of your stomach, what I and many people call your soul spot or your soul's place. There was an amazing aura, power about him. His manner of speech – eloquent. His audience manner – capture the eyes

157

and hold them long enough to get a reaction and then move on.

You could tell from the look of enchantment and awe on the faces of so many in the room that he was succeeding in making them feel like the room was empty, and he was speaking directly to them - one on one. With just the sound of his voice he seemed to be shaking hands individually with every man in the room. At the same time touching the most intimate emotions of every woman. It was haunting. This felt like more than receiving Godly confirmation through a preached word, this was listen to my voice and you will hear what you've been looking for.

"Warren, do you ever go to church?"

"Yeah, why?"

"Is it strange to you that his whole presentation thus far has been all about him?"

"I don't get it. He's talking about his role as a preacher."

"No, he's talking about how you're supposed to give your life in service to the preacher. He said, 'no man can serve two masters'; and that is why leaders in First Alliance must spend an intense time in life re-direction. That piece of scripture actually means you can't worship God and act like the Devil, and while it is re-directing the focus of your life – it's not quite the way he's presenting it."

"Makes sense though, he's in the Bible; but he's subtly changing your thought pattern."

"Exactly."

I set my attention back on the sermon as Warren rose to answer his vibrating cell phone. Moving in and out quietly he said one of his co-workers had come up on something interesting happening on one of the floors the church had rented and they were going to check it out. Not wanting to leave me alone, he urged me to come along. While walking to the car parked on the second level; Warren and I barely escaped being plowed down by a car backing out of a parking spot. Pulling me up from the ground, Warren pointed out several men dragging a young girl into a van. While hearing them clearly was not an option above the sound of the car's still screeching tires; we did hear enough to know that they were leaders with the church. I could tell from the look on Warren's face that he was concerned about what was going on and his level of concern became more evident when he told me to go back into the hotel and look for a particular gentleman.

"Warren I don't like this. You're obviously tripping about what's going on with them and that van, and you are not – I repeat are not leaving me here."

"Look Crystal. This is not TV. I am not your husband. Right now, my protecting you means not taking you wherever in the hell they're going. Now I'm going to call Jay and tell him to meet you at the check in desk. He's wearing a black shirt and pants, and a Star of David. You can't miss him. He's about six five and looks like he weighs twenty pounds. Please stay here and find him."

For the first time in this whole ordeal I found myself agreeing with Anthony, maybe I was in way over my head. Maybe this was not where I needed to be. Maybe I should have sat my behind home and waited for him to get back. But no. Not me. I'm Crystal – I can do what I want. Confused and scared, all I wanted to do was cry; and so, as

I waited for the elevator that is what I did - cried. That's when a familiar face appeared from behind the slowly opening elevator doors. It was Nisa or as Warren and Anthony knew her, Nujara.

"Auntie Crys what's wrong? Did someone hurt you? What's wrong?"

Nisa pulled me away from the elevator and into the stairwell. As we settled ourselves on the stairs, she wiped tears from my face with a bandana she always kept tied on her arm. She said someone gave it to her one night and she felt better with it close to her.

"What are you doing here, Nisa?"

"Ant's flight got delayed. He couldn't get you on your cell and he said something about he couldn't find the other number for some guy you were supposed to be with. He wanted me to come find you guys and let you know. Where is the guy?"

"Strangest thing just happened in the parking lot. First, we almost got ran down and then these men threw this girl in a van. I think he followed them. Nisa, please as God lives and reigns tell me what is going on here."

The evil that tempts me

Chapter Twelve

I was very clearly putting Nisa on the spot. There was no question about that; but I could not take any more of this just wait foolishness. I was scared out of my mind. I was mad at everything and everybody. I was 10 seconds away from a nervous breakdown in a very well-kept hotel stairwell; and I felt like I was walking around in one big nightmare and everybody else was awake around me going "ssh, ssh don't wake her up."

"Nisa! Nujara...."

She rose quickly running several stairs away from where I sat. "Don't ever call me that. It's a name with no purpose. It's the name of a dead person."

I felt sorry for her. I didn't mean to hurt her. I just wanted her to understand that I was at a point of desperation now. I needed to know something, anything, everything and I needed to know now.

"Auntie Crys, my Uncle loves you so. If you get mad at him after I tell you this stuff, I would never forgive myself and Pastor Thompson, well.... just keep loving him, okay."

"Do I have a reason to stop loving him Nisa? Is finding out like this that you married somebody that had a whole life that you don't have any clue about reason enough to stop loving somebody? Is finding out like this that your husband never trusted you enough to tell you about this foolishness before now, enough to stop loving some-body? And did I just hear you say that my husband is your uncle? Anthony is your uncle? What is going on here?"

Holding me in an effort to comfort me; Nisa was cry-ing even harder than I was. She knew that out of every one involved in this drama, I was the one on stage with no script and therefore was lost as to the beginning, immersed in a rapidly moving production with no directions and headed for a dangerous ending. Nisa finally began to put the pieces together. The story she shared was beautiful, sad and left me even more confused about my husband.

Anthony had a sister, Darmisha. She was Nisa's mother. Anthony also once dated a woman that Thomp-son was madly in love with. The problem was Anthony was also very much in love with this woman and did everything he could creatively think of to keep Thomp-son from sleeping with her. Nisa said Thompson hated Anthony because of that relationship. He felt betrayed by him. Two days after her seventeenth birthday, she died of cancer – at least that was what the congregation was told. Nisa said she remembers going to the farewell service and seeing Anthony watch through a window crying.

"Why was he watching from the window?"

"Pastor told him he would kill him if he stepped foot in the service. I remember my momma holding him and telling him not to cry – we would all be okay one day."

"You said she died of cancer, but you don't sound like you really believe that."

"None of the leaders in the church ever gave you a cause of death – this was only one of a few times they did. Anthony and my mom, at the time, thought she might have killed herself; and to avoid taking any blame for it, Thompson ordered people to say she died of cancer."

"I don't understand."

"I heard mom and Uncle Ant talking one night .... seems Pastor Thompson really may have cared for this girl. She came into the church willingly. She immediately started working on every council. All I really remember about her, was she had this beautiful, long, wavy black hair and she always sang when she worked - His eye is on the sparrow. I remember Ant's eyes from the window. I think the only other time I saw that much pain in some- one was the last time I saw my mother."

"I am so sorry baby." I pulled Nisa to me and held her for a moment and then she pulled away, wiping tears from her lovely, beige eyes.

While Anthony had found a place in his heart and his spirit not to be afraid of Thompson; he knew that betraying him about that specific matter probably would not get him killed or hurt; but would mean harm to Nisa and Darmisha. She continued to explain that Thompson was convinced Anthony was saving Lashira for him- self – which would have been fine – except the rule was Pastor slept with every woman before you married her. Nisa didn't know why. She assumed that it was his way of testing a woman's spirit. Two months after Lashira died Anthony walked away. No one knew how he did it. But

165

he did. While Thompson never went looking for him, he began to rape Nisa's mother regularly.

Finally, one day after conceiving Thompson's second child during three months of high holy days and being taunted by the church leaders – the same leaders that encouraged her to nourish the pastor; she decided she couldn't take it anymore and she tried to kill herself. She didn't succeed at suicide, but she did terminate the pregnancy. That too enraged Thompson, and he sent her away to the church in New Jersey. Shortly after that Anthony would start appearing at Thompson's restaurant, which sat right behind the New Jersey sanctuary. He would slide his sister phone numbers and leave. It was easier there, because no one had seen him for five years and people there didn't really know him. By this time, Nisa was 13.

"Nisa, is this man looking for Anthony to kill him? Will he kill him?"

She kept talking like I had never opened my mouth. She just cupped my hands in her much smaller and lighter complexioned ones and squeezed. "One day, out of nowhere, me and mom were told to stop working. Well, they told her to stop working. She was cooking. I was cropping greens; the younger ones did stuff like that. I still remember she was frying pork chops for the restaurant. She made the best pork chops."

I rambled through my purse and found a sheet of tissue or two, one for Nisa and one for me. "Stay focused baby. I promised Warren, I'd find some tall guy wearing a Star of David."

"We didn't even go back to our apartment. We got in a car and they took us back to Akron. Our first night there,

Mother Adele came to our room and told mama that
she had been selected to marry co-Pastor Myunara. Oh,
my God, Crys I didn't understand a lot of it, but mama's
whole body was shaking like Jell-O, and she started
sweating. And her eyes did this strange thing, they looked
like glass."

Nisa said her mother knew not to cry for fear of being
disciplined. And she knew to just sit there quietly, and not
let them see her snatching looks in her mother's direction. Mother Adele, not ready to deal with the disappoint-
ment and pain standing before her, turned away from
Darmisha, and completed her instructions. Darmisha
should get herself together to see the pastor. That night, to
prepare for her new husband, she would have to supply
spiritual nourishment to the pastor.

"When Mother Adele left, mama changed suddenly.
She didn't look scared anymore. She didn't look anything
bad, or sad, nothing like what I thought was her being
mad enough to kill somebody. That's what I saw - death
in her eyes. She was light and cheerful. She was dancing
around with me. 'Come my little muffin, dance with me.'
We danced and danced, then she decided to make our
home a place for the light. She said as place for the light.

Moments later, after changing around furniture,
mopping, sweeping and dusting, Darmisha put on one
of her celebration robes. A fitting, but long red and gold
African print dress and she wrapped her thick braids in
a matching scarf. Nisa said her mother kissed her on the
cheek and embraced her for several moments before she
left, whispering quietly in her ear. 'You are more than this
muffin. This is not of God and He will rescue you. You are

my light and I love you.' She says that was the last time she saw her mother.

On occasion Nisa said some of the girls would go into town with the older women to purchase feminine items. The women were not as vigilant in watching every single move as the deacons were. There were times when Nisa would sneak to a phone and call Anthony. The last call she made to him was to tell him she was being prepared to nourish the Pastor. Together they decided she had to leave; but before they could work things out she was forced to rejoin the group when she noticed one of the deacons gathering the flock.

Darmisha, after nourishing the pastor for quite some time, decided she needed to rid herself of the filth that had invaded her. She was given permission to go back to her own apartment, after saying she wanted to make sure things were unpacked and settled in properly before worship service the next morning and before receiving her new husband.

"Right after mama left, Sister Rosaura and three other ladies I didn't know came for me. I cried and fell on the ground and grabbed hold to whatever I could. I kept asking for mama and they kept telling me to stop acting like a child, and to shut up – this behavior is of not of God. They were yelling all kinds of orders at me." Nisa grabbed her head in her hand as those she could hear them again. So, I reached to embrace her, but my touch startled her.

"They just gave me to some other woman, an older mother in church. She said she was to give me instructions in being a young woman and a servant leader. They would never tell me where my mother was, or if I would see her."

I watched this beautiful young woman wilt into a dark place, and I couldn't let her continue this. My selfish curiosity had taken her into a hell, I'm sure she had hoped she never visit again.

"Hey, listen, let's just go back to my house and I'll make us something hot to eat. You don't have to tell me anything else. I shouldn't have pushed you this far." I reached out my hand and took a step down the stairwell. She grabbed my hand, and I exhaled. The air of relief halted when she pulled me back to the cold slab to sit.

"Let me just finish. I need to finish for me this time. Okay?"

Though they were on the same compound, for two days prior to her death, Darmisha and Nisa had not seen each other. On the first Sunday of the next month, Nisa was bathed and robed to be with the Pastor. The new ones or the first nourishers of the pastor and weddings were always on baptismal Sunday.

"When he touched my breasts, oh God, I felt like needles were sticking me. I stepped back and tripped over the chair. He grabbed me and …."

"Nisa, don't it's okay."

"He started licking me from my breast to my navel. And I was shaking. He liked that." I closed my eyes hoping the tears wouldn't spill out into yells. How I hated that bastard at that moment. "I started pushing him away, trying to move his head away from me. And he kinda threw me on to the bed. He just kept trying Auntie Crys, he just

kept trying and I didn't know what to do, so I yelled –
DADDY! DADDY, DON'T DO THIS!"

"Warren told me about that, I don't... But he said your
stepfather walked in on him raping you and that he found
your mother, well...."

"She slit her wrists. My mama had been on kind of
– restriction phase – my stepfather wasn't supposed to
come back. There was some confusion or something,
that's why she was being given to a co-pastor. After her
time of preparation with the Pastor, which started Friday
night and went through Saturday night, mama came back
to our room to check on things and I guess from what I
could figure out, took her last bath. I never knew what
happened to my stepfather after that."

Nisa later found a note explaining what had been
happening to her mother. The note was a written prayer
to God. She was repenting for allowing herself to be so
weak that she would not flee from "the evil that tempts
me and controls my life". She asked that God send His
angels to take her child to a safer place; "a place of salvation, deliverance and peace". She prayed that her brother
would never be as weak as she was and would not return
to this place. The last line in the prayer, simply said,
"while I ask you Lord to forgive me for being weak, I even
at this moment, still am not strong. And so, on this night,
I have decided to be with you. I cannot protect my daughter from this. I know in my heart that her turn is quickly
approaching. Maybe if she stands in mourning, they will
overlook her at least for a while."

Moments later, Darmisha would step into a bathtub
full of water and rose petals; her braids tied up in a simple

red bandana and do what was necessary to take her own life. When her estranged husband, who was supposed to be on his way to Miami, walked into the room about an hour later, Nisa said she heard people say that he fell to his knees throwing up and screaming damnation to Thompson. When he saw the prayer that her mother had left, he knew that Nisa was in trouble. With hatred and fear filling every part of his being, he rushed into Thompson's private chambers. He probably expected to find Nisa, but certainly not the way he did. Nisa said he came in while she was screaming from the force pounding her body. He pulled Thompson from behind her and out of her re-violated and battered loins; her mother's blood still on his hands.

Anthony had come back to get Nisa and Darmisha. Her mother had called him in the twinkling hours of Saturday morning, prior to Nisa's rites of passage, from the pastor's room while he was in the shower. She had apparently shared with Anthony some of the things she shared in her last letter to God. He, didn't catch his sister's resolve to die rather than continue to live like she had been doing; so, he figured he'd risk his life and just walk in there and take them both out. By the time he got there, it was clear, all hell had broken loose. He saw a group of men dragging and beating Nisa's stepfather in one direction; while a group of women carried, what seemed to be a lifeless body, in another direction. He followed the women knowing it had to have been Nisa or Darmisha. Someone following him forced him to change his running path and for a time he hid, losing track. That's how Nisa ended up with the old woman whom she and Anthony both began to call Auntie and that's how she ended up in Miami. Anthony found Nisa because he knew she could not have gotten far and would daily, for almost a week, search the woods for her. When he realized that the comfort his 'aunt' could provide for her was more than a man could at that point; he opted to leave her there. He and Nisa told this woman everything; and in her heart of compassion she covered them like only a mother could, and nursed Nisa back to sanity.

"So, Pastor Thompson is your father and he's Anthony's godfather? But if Anthony and your mother..."

"No, that's what really is probably killing pastor about Anthony getting away and about his life now. Pastor Thompson is Ant's father too. Ant is his first-born son. But he's not his wife's son. Anthony and my mom share the same mother and father. My grandmother killed herself during labor trying not to let Anthony be born. She apparently told pastor's wife that neither of them would live in the evil they were creating. But Anthony didn't die. The woman that raised him and my mother until pastor took him at 12 was just a leader in the church."

"Warren said that he and Anthony think Cathy English was using me to get to Anthony. Lashay, that's what Warren called her."

"Lashay is Thompson and I think Mother Adele's daughter. She probably is. But then she may not be. Lashay was never quite right in the head. One minute she was one way, the next minute – woo woo – she was off in lala land."

Suddenly a door to a stairway above us opened and three men approached us. From behind them I could see Cathy English. And I recognized one of the men as Thompson. He himself now stood before us. His power was so amazingly strong, so frightening, so evil that Nisa wet her pants and I felt tears falling from my eyes and a massive stirring in my soul spot. They stopped at the top of the stairway and watched us as though we were to recognize that we were being beckoned. Nisa clung to me, as though if she let go she would lose her life.

"I'm sorry, we got a little lost trying to get to the parking lot, but we'll move aside so that you can get past us."

Quietly, I started praying that the look of familiarity on their face and the lack of the same look on my mine would force them to simply walk past us. But it didn't. So rather than wait for this obvious moment of reckoning; I gathered my purse from the floor, grabbed Nisa by the waist and made a quick dash for the door. As swiftly as I moved, so did the two men that were with Cathy and Thompson, and before I knew what was happening, we were pushed into a hotel room. Nisa knew one thing when confronted with Thompson's crew and empty rooms and that was fight, and so she began to do just that, both of us realizing that the last thing we wanted was to hear the door close. So, we fought like we were kicking down the gates of hell to keep them from closing that door. Nails, fists, legs, teeth – if it was on us – we employed whatever we were like weapons against them. Cathy tried to console us; to warn us to allow the moment to happen.

"Please Mrs. Houston, Nujara stop this. Stop this. You're going to make things worse. Please Pastor just wants to talk you."

"Shut up and get out of my way. You grab me in a stairway and throw me in a room and we are supposed to believe you just want to talk. Oh no. We will fight up in here this day."

I back-handed Cathy sending her into a hallway wall. A lovely oriental vase with silk flowers crashed beside her. Nisa made a dash for the door and as I tried to follow her someone pulled me back into the room. Pushing me into a chair like a child that had been misbehaving, Thompson cut a glance at me that warned me to be still.

"You really need to calm down. Did you not hear Lashay say that I only want to talk to you? I just need to sit and get to know you." He directed his attention to one of the men, who moved at the urging in Thompson's eyes.

"You only want me because you're looking for my husband. You are a very sick and dangerous man. Now Nisa knows I'm in here, so does a detective – I suggest you let me out this room; and I suggest you do it now!"

"You are in no position to make any demands here. And Deacon Ross will catch up with Nisa."

That he did. Before Thompson could go on, Nisa was thrown back into the room by the gentleman I presumed was Deacon Ross. He also very nonchalantly dragged Cathy into the room and pushed the door closed behind him. Surely, I thought with all the noise up here, someone had to have called hotel security. Someone must have figured out there was something out of the norm going on and prayerfully they cared enough to call the police. I couldn't imagine what Warren must have walked into but at this moment, I wanted him to walk into this room. I wouldn't have even minded if Jay, whoever that was walked into this room – I just knew that we needed help. Oh God, I heard my sub-conscious screaming, why didn't I listen to Anthony? Why didn't I believe him or Warren about how dangerous this man was?

You wanna play
preacher,

let's play

Chapter Thirteen

It felt like hours had past, although, realistically, I'm sure it had only been about fifteen minutes and no one was looking for us. The horror of all the stories Warren had told me and Nisa's memories began to march around in my gut. Like an army of consciousness, her memories, and my nightmares ranted in my head, screaming "didn't he say you don't know what you are getting into." They marched in formation, the little army of fear, uncertainty and disbelief. Now what was I going to do? Not only was I in trouble now, but I had managed to get Nisa in a tragic situation. I found myself crying for her. What pain all of this must be bringing back.

Deacon Ross stood like a tree watching nothing but periodically searching Thompson's face for some type of instruction. Then his eyes would slowly move from woman to woman. What was it? Was he trying to make sure we were all okay? Was he contemplating if this would be a time of nourishment for Thompson and he was imagining which one of us would be first? Did he even care, I thought, in a moment of anger, that all of this is wrong?

If he thought anything it certainly did not show on his face. His face had about as much emotion as the autumn flowers colored couch that sat in this hotel room. I could not see the face of the other man because for the most part he kept his face turned away from us, occasionally placing his ear against the door. I assumed he was listening for any indication that the police had in fact been called. Cathy English just fiddled with everything. She was like a nervous child caught shoplifting at the corner store. Nisa would not stop crying.

"Nujara, you are as beautiful as your mother was. You are blessed, so blessed. You have grown to be pleasing to the sight."

It was sickening the way he watched her. I thought about Nisa just barely a teenager having to be prepared to sleep with and then repeatedly raped by her own father. I found myself whispering a prayer of comfort. Praying that at this very moment, God would protect her from those memories. The last time she was this close to this man, her father, he had taken her virginity. Here in this place, the scared girl that peed her pants moments earlier and then allowed her fear to force her to fight for her life suddenly through tears and trails of snot found a new courage. It certainly had to rise from the bottom of her feet, through her intestines, through her esophagus and into the healthy wad of spit that landed squarely on his nose.

He raised his hand to slap her, when Nisa again started swinging and so I did the same. This time however Thompson decided that this may not be the location to force whatever he wanted to happen. I could hear him yell for one of the men to put Nisa in the bedroom and then both needed to get some cases and a car. As they exited the room they took Cathy with them. I fell to the floor crying, praying that God would cover me in my stupidity that he would send someone to get me.

"Get up child. I am not going to hurt you. I want to talk to you about your husband..."

Without warning, my prayers were strangely and quickly answered. The door obviously did not close soundly, because just as Thompson bent over to pull me up from the floor, Anthony pushed the door opened.

"My wife has nothing to say to you, especially about me."

Thompson loosed his grip on my arm and turned to face the voice behind him. There was a smug look on his face and there was the look of a man willing to fight on Anthony. It was a look that I had never seen him wear and one that chilled me.

"Michael. It's been a long time. "

Anthony never acknowledged the name Thompson called him instead he walked past him, picked me up and assured that I was okay.

"Have you seen Nisa?"

I motioned to the bedroom with my head and Anthony nodded and asked me to get her. Calmly assuring me that we were about to leave.

"Michael there is no reason to alarm the woman like that."

"My name is not Michael, but surely LaShay has told you that."

"Your mother named you after the archangel...."

"My mother didn't name me anything. That was a name you put on me, hoping that I would walk in your sick behind image of an archangel."

"Watch yourself boy. You owe me the res…"

"Shit man, I don't owe you anything. What respect? The respect of a father? No, you raped my mother, you hid her away and kept raping her until she killed herself and tried to take me with her. The respect of what a preacher? You and I both know there's no God in anything you're doing. The respect of what a man? No, no can't be that – you aren't man enough to discipline people in your own sick fantasy world. You aren't man enough to sleep with grown women, you prefer little girls. What you figure I owe you man – what? Huh? Truth is you're scared. People are talking now. They wouldn't do that before."

"You need to learn to shut up. I'm in control of this damn situation here boy. I can shut down this whole conference right now and take all three of you all out of here and they'll never see you again."

"Then do it man. Do it. DO IT! I'm not scared of you man and I can assure you, that before I let you hurt my niece and my wife, you'll be covered in blood and not the blood of Jesus. You wanna play preacher – let's play."

Nisa and I stood trembling against the bedroom door. Part of me wanted to run for help. Part of me was afraid to leave. Nisa must have sensed my concern. She squeezed me I guess when she assumed the moment was right for us to move and she darted past Anthony and Thompson. Anthony looked past Thompson's thick stature to where

I stood as though asking, 'why didn't you go with her?' I crept to where he stood; afraid to approach him. Afraid to leave him.

"Anthony, please let's go. Please don't let him pull you in to anything."

"I'm fine Crys. Go with Nisa, get in the car and go to Warren's."

"Nobody's going anywhere Michael. You owe me boy. You plucked a flower out of my garden and I haven't been able to find anyone like her since you did."

"What are you talking about man? My mother..."

"Come on boy – your mother didn't mean a damn thing to me, she didn't want to fulfill her role as a female leader..."

"Nigger, I will hurt you. Dare you stand there and tell me you didn't feel anything for my mother. You man, will always be the reason I don't know her. Fine, you not talking about my mother who - Darmisha, Nisa, Kahira, who? Which woman do you think I plucked from your garden?"

"You know who I am talking about, Lashira. Your wife knows about Lashira?"

"My wife doesn't know anything about ... "

"Oh, you weren't man enough to tell her where you come from. I guess I'm not the only one you need to get some things right with huh."

"I don't have to get anything right with you. Lashira was a beautiful woman. And I loved her with my life. And if we had found each other in other circumstances I probably would be with her today. Then again maybe I wouldn't be. I'm where God would have me to be."

Hearing what Anthony was saying sent me to another place. I was confused and I questioned if this man really loved me for me or if I was simply replacing his first love. I slowly raised my eyes to see Anthony's face. Was there something in his eyes at this moment that would tell me if I was just tripping? What I got was again a look of concern and an urging to get out of harm's way. Anthony pushed me away from him and towards the door, pressing the car keys in my hand. He watched Thompson like he had to be vigilant about his presence. I moved towards the door sensing the anger between the two of them rising and filling the space.

"You messed up something boy. You messed up something powerful. That girl moved me in a way you didn't understand. I was going to marry her. She was going to be the first lady that was going to help me take this church to heights you can't even imagine for a ministry."

"This is not ministry man and Shira never would have married you. We studied together. We talked. She knew this was false religion. She didn't respect you as a preacher. Her spirit stayed so sweet because she knew the true God – she loved him enough to love everybody in that situation – despite what was going on."

"It was that foolishness you were putting in her head that made her kill herself."

"Kill herself...Adele told me that wasn't true. She said Shira really was sick."

"Adele is sometimes a foolish woman. She loved you like a son and it broke her heart when you left. And Fujana, lie after lie after lie. You beat her up and ran away.

You stole all her stuff and ran away. Come to find out she was too busy screwing Satan to notice you were simply walking away. You were good, for a long time I thought you were dead. Figured you were weak like your mother and your sister."

"Come on man, you've obviously been watching me, watching Crystal. Lashay's been your eyes and your ears, so you should know you can't get me that way. Suicide is not an option for me; but hey if that's your thing, do what you gotta do. I don't believe you about Lashira by the way."

"Oh, please do, Lashira killed herself.… looked me in my eyes, cursed me, prayed for you, then slit her throat. Prayed for your behind and all I was trying to do was love her. Love her like a woman should be loved. I mean after all you hadn't been man enough to receive her nourishment."

"No, I was man enough to wait for it to be offered. I didn't have to rape women I'd fathered to get mine."

Reaching for the door knob after lingering long enough to hear the chorus of past hurt and current hate reach a crescendo; I heard the crash of a fist on skin and the sound of a body falling over something. Looking back, I watched Anthony rising from the couch where he landed and Thompson lunged toward him. Anthony hit him directly in the abdomen stopping his movement. I fell against the hotel wall; in my head I was yelling STOP! Anthony STOP! Please baby don't do this. But there was no sound. I watched them fight feeling like I was right in the middle of one of those nightmares again. I was reaching for him and he didn't reach back. I never moved from the wall. The keys were in my hands and my mind was yelling and I was reaching for Anthony. In my mind. In my mind.

"Come on old man. You gotta come harder than that. Oh, but I forgot...." Anthony slapped him with the back of his hand across the left cheek knocking him across the chair that sat beneath the desk. "You aren't used to doing your own hitting are you man. Let me show you how it's done. How about you feel what you been ordering dished out."

"You always did talk too much boy. If you got something for me throw it. Come on boy."

Anthony played with him almost, it seemed, tickling his chin with fingers, then he slapped his right cheek with the back of his hand. While Thompson struggled for balance, Anthony pulled his favorite leather belt from about his waist and hit Thompson on the back again and again and again. Thompson, through the swings of the belt, would land blows but nothing hard enough to stop Anthony's fury.

"No line of deacons to help you now old man huh? What kind of ass-whooping you due man? How much chastisement man? My mother. Darmisha. Lashira. How much man, huh?"

I knew he must have been beating him for the old and the new; yet the enraged animal that he was at this moment chilled me. In my mind, the thing that controlled him was as sick as the thing that had prompted Thompson's actions all these years. Finally, I heard me yelling. I kept yelling for him to stop. Yelling for him to calm down. But he wouldn't. He couldn't because Thompson just kept taunting him like he was trying to drive him crazy. He kept swinging. He kept swinging ... and so ... he didn't hear me screaming and I didn't see him crying. All I could see was the hate that he was wearing. Inside he obviously was being torn all apart - again. Warren, Jay and Nisa burst through the door – it took both men to pull Anthony from him.

"You happy old man? Huh? This is what you wanted right? You wanted to find out if I was scared of you. If I would fight you, right? Well now you know."

Thompson touched his face, his arms, and his back feeling the cuts from the belt all over his body. Again, he lunged at Anthony – the barrel of Jay's gun in his face stopping him in his tracks. Anthony pulled away from Warren and fell to his knees after taking only a few small steps from Thompson's battered frame. Nisa fell to the floor next to him pulling him towards her, holding him like I have never seen two people hold each other. Warren turned to face me and I could tell from his expression that he wondered why it wasn't me crying at his side. I couldn't move. I didn't know the man that belonged to this story. I didn't know the man who had just exploded in rage before me. I could understand the reason for the rage, after all of these weeks, after all of these years, but I could not understand – I couldn't even name what it was I had just seen. The key I gripped in my hand pierced my skin. I watched the blood drip to the carpeted floor, turned and walked out.

Anthony caught me in the stairwell crying and throwing up. I felt so incredibly tired. I was empty - hollow but pained at the same time. I didn't know what to do but hold

on to the rail and purge whatever was boiling within me.
I didn't want to feel secure from the stroking of Anthony's
hands on my back. I couldn't even begin to put words to
what I felt for him or about him in that very instance.

"I don't know who you are."

He pulled me away from the rail and tried to bring
me close to him. I resisted and fell back against the wall,
the smell of vomit and sweat mixing in my nostrils. It was
truth, I did not know who this man was.

"Crystal listen to me. I am Anthony Houston. I am the
Anthony you've been with all these years. I am the man
God has told you I am."

"You're that man's son. His blood is in your veins, in
me...."

"No baby. I am not his son. I have one father, and He
is Lord. One father Crys. I know baby, I know I must have
scared you in there, but you gotta believe..."

"Believe what? You? Who do I believe Michael,
Anthony, who?"

"I have not been Michael Thompson since the day
I caught a bus out of Atlanta headed to California. I am
Anthony Houston and everything that he is, you know.
Crystal..."

I pushed him away from me and started a sprint down
the stairs and through the door that led to the parking
garage. Part of me wanted him to chase me. I was mad. I
was jealous. Surely, he would have run after Lashira. Part
of me wanted him to stay in the stinky stairwell and think
about how he'd torn my heart out of my chest. I climbed
into my truck and poured my soul out on the steering
wheel. Afraid to leave but more afraid to stay.

Those persecuted for
Christ's sake

Chapter Fourteen

I felt sorry for whoever had the pleasure of cleaning up room 234 in the Marriott Courtyard that day. It was a mess, urine and blood and sweat. Two months after a series of altercations on so many levels that nearly destroyed my faith in God, my faith in people and my faith in my husband - Thompson was indicted and sent to trial on numerous charges including sexual battery, assault, attempted murder, kidnapping and racketeering. This time there were dozens of people who were members and leaders that came forward. Between Anthony and Warren, they had convinced them that their voices combined would be the only way to send him away for a lengthy period. Throughout the trial there were bits of hard testimony; one of the witnesses was Thompson's former daughter-in-law. Janine Davis, Mohana, as she was called in the church told a story that filled me with sadness.

The bailiff swore her in. "For the record, please state your full name."

"My name is Janine Davis."

Thompson leaned in to the sharply dressed female attorney that led his defense team. Slim, dark skinned, with long wavy natural hair and striking figures. She had a confidence that did not seem to fit her. Still, she came out swinging.

"Ms. Davis. I've checked the church membership information for several years, and don't see your name listed."

"My name when I was in the – when I was there, was Mohana."

"The only Mohana I show, is listed as deceased."

"Mohana is dead, figuratively. She was reclaimed as the woman she was born as – Janine Davis."

"I see from my information here that you have been under psychiatric care for several years."

"I began seeing a counselor shortly after I escaped, and do see one occasionally when the nightmares are prominent."

"Mohana..."

"Janine. Janine Davis."

"You indicated you escaped, but the truth of the matter is you kidnapped a child from the Akron residential plaza. Isn't that correct?"

A prosecuting attorney, interrupted the line of questioning. "Your honor, I'm going to have to object. Counsel indicated that she shows Mohana is dead in court records and now she's accusing the same person of kidnapping – is there more than one person with the same name?"

She glanced back at Thompson, not for instruction but almost apologetically. The judge agreeing with the prosecutor. "For sake of clarity counselor, are there two

Mohanas and if there is only one clarify which line of questioning you will pursue."

She stepped quickly to the table and thumbed through a folder before offering an explanation. "The kidnapping that I referenced was five years before the person is noted as deceased. It is likely the same person and the notation of death may have been an error in my office, your honor. I would like to request a few moments your honor to confer with my office and assure that I have presented the court with accurate information."

"Your honor, I don't mind a recess in the matter, however it is approaching the lunch time you have indicated for the jury, and I would like the opportunity to briefly question Ms. Davis before then." Her stall tactic did not work, and the deep breath from Thompson's side of the defense table spoke volumes.

"My husband and the pastor had an argument one night that left him, Pastor Thompson, insane with rage. I had never seen him that mad. I was scared. For hours, I begged James to apologize. I told him things could get dangerous. Finally, he said he would. He left the house saying that he would do it right then. I was so relieved. Two hours after he left the house, two deacons dragged him bleeding and full of open wounds into the house. My baby was four, and he looked at his father and started screaming that there was a monster in the house. That's how swollen and bruised his face was – he didn't even look like himself."

Mohana testified that during the night James died quietly in his sleep. She didn't know if he had in fact been beaten to death or if his heart had broken from his relationship with his father, the truths about the church and his desire to leave it; or maybe she said his heart and his lungs simply gave out from the weight of his anxiety.

"He, Thompson, blamed me. All the leaders in the church blamed me. They took me and my baby and made us live in a room above the barn. They just left us there. It was cold and he kept crying. After two nights of no food, and the crying, and having to sleep behind barrels to block the wind at night, I knew I had to do something. The temperature was dropping and we were going to die in there."

"Who was aware that you were in this room above the barn? Who ordered that you be placed there?" The prosecutor kept his gaze on the jurors as he posed the question. Two women jurors wiped tears away.

"Adelle, Thompson's wife came with them and said that the pastor was very disappointed that I did not care for my husband properly. That my unconcern killed him. She said I, and Isaiah had to endure 30 days of confinement. All the leaders knew where we were. They didn't let me take any clothes, toys, food, nothing."

One morning as the kids were gathered for school, Mohana said she wrapped her ailing son in a blanket used for the cows and jumped from a second story window. She said her baby clung to her, holding on to her shoulders so tight that he tore the skin on one spot. When she heard the dogs bark, she realized it would only be seconds before they noticed what was happening, so she ran. She ran through a section of woods behind the barn that was not fenced off and ended at a heavily-used road. When she reached the road, a white couple in a pick-up truck nearly hit her. They gathered her and her son in the back of the truck and drove them to a hospital in the next town. When she was assured her son was fine, she bundled him in some things that had been donated by the couple and some nurses, called her parents in Miami and waited for them to come get her. She said it took her five minutes to get beyond hello when she called, because she suddenly found herself unable to do or say anything. All she could do was cry and because she cried her mother did the same on the other end. It was her father's voice trembling that finally brought resolution to the purpose for the call.

"He said, I'm coming baby. You go back to that hospital and you stay there until I get there. He must've drove non-stop. We waited for him in the emergency room. When I looked up and saw him and my mama, I fainted."

The rest of the case centered on correlations to other cults and how cults are a combination of a lot of things … but primarily elements of extreme control, extreme discipline, and extreme spiritual bondage. After some of the most horrific court testimony I'd ever heard, including Warren's and Anthony's. Thompson was found guilty and sentenced to life in prison. Anthony's testimony on the day the case went to the jury perhaps put things in perspective for anyone that found the other testimonies far-fetched. The attorney asked him to explain as best he could why First Alliance could function as long as it did.

"I have asked myself that same question repeatedly. I wanted to know how women I'd heard spoken of and had met in this church could or would allow themselves to be used and abused the way they were. I asked myself why men would stand with an air of honor and watch the 'man of God' physically, emotionally, mentally and sexually abuse women - some who they would be given as wives. Some they would just be allowed to use as temporary whores - even I at 15, 16, 17 had the privilege. It happened, people stayed, people fled and came back because this man found a way to build an almost inde-structible kingdom based on inferiority, esteem murder, secrets and sexual and criminal acts that he could hold over people. Then he topped it all off by destroying the one thing that can make you get up when everything else is gone - your spirit.

Once he found a way to defeat and even kill your spirit, using the very thing that is the foundation of the world – and that's God - you were not leaving. Sadly, for most of the women - suicide was the only way to escape what they had walked into believing and hoping that it was the answer to troubling life situations. You are told and convinced that your family does not want you and will never receive you again - because he'll tell them what you've been involved in. You never think that if you can hold it over my head, it truly was not of God. Then there were so many like me. Born into it with nowhere else to go. So, you stay and you wait on God and you serve the pastor as wrong as he is. It succeeded for the same reason slavery did - we didn't know initially that we were slaves and then too many of us fought against freedom. You destroy a people not from the outside in, but from the inside out and that's what William Thompson did."

Anthony told the court that he had had the opportu-nity several times over the years to help people walk away and to assure them that there was real life in a real God and that even with all that they had seen in First Alliance they could still find a place of true worship and true deliverance. He testified that the woman he knew as his mother until he was taken away at 12 chose to stay inside First Alliance so that she could "set free the caged birds".

When he knew that Thompson would stand trial and probably figure out that she'd known all along where he was and that she had helped many leave quietly the way he did; he made one last visit to the Akron compound to get her. Now safe in protective custody, her deposition revealed and confirmed so much about the techniques used to prepare young women to nourish the pastor. It also revealed that if one took a fancy to total the number of children Thompson had fathered - it would be close to 95. She revealed that Thompson had a disdain for women, because he discovered early in his own marriage that his wife's body would not respond to his touch. Of the eight children, they raised as their own, only two were birthed by her. The defense attorney drilled Anthony based on the allegations revealed in the deposition that left the room void of air and spirit.

"Have you ever actually witnessed any of these alleged sexual assaults?"

"The first one I saw I was 12. I remember seeing the girl a couple of days before doing hair on the porch of one of the mothers; she couldn't have been more than 15."

"Why didn't you report it?"

"To whom? The pastor who was raping her or the deacon who told me to watch and then went in the room to get his piece handled?"

"Isn't it true Mr. Houston, that you actually took part in what you are now calling rape sessions?"

"When I was 15, I lost my virginity to two women; one my age and one older that told us what to do and when to do it. Several times after that I had the opportunity, sometimes I took it, sometimes I didn't. But as far as anyone knew we were sexing and stroking and everything else."

"What do you mean as far as anyone knew?"

"If the elders or Pastor ever thought that we were not doing anything, then they would consider the girls disobedient and they would be beaten. I know this because the first time I told a deacon I didn't want to sleep with this girl, Uhara - they beat her. The last time I saw her I was 16 and she was still walking with a limp. I didn't want to sleep with her because she was only 12. So, if all we did was fall asleep, I told them we had sex."

"Were you ever beaten?"

"No."

"Did you ever actually witness any beatings?"

"No, just the after effects."

"How do you know it wasn't a simple fight, a bar brawl if you will?"

"Then it was a whole lot of simple, unfair fights."

"I'm sorry."

"Unfair fights. If 12 men wearing plastic overalls are waiting for you with weapons in their hands when you walk in a room, that's an unfair fight. That's assault if I'm not mistaken."

"Isn't it true Mr. Houston, that you are merely testifying today and that you deliberately went after Pastor Thompson because he has cut you from his will?"

Anthony laughed loudly and for several moments, before the judged warned him and reminded him that he was still under oath.

"Look man. I walked away from Thompson's main concubine while she was getting hers with another pastor in a hotel room. A day and half later I was in Pasadena. Three days after that I met a lawyer at Legal Aid, told him my story and I had a new identity. For a year, I went to day school and night school to get a legal diploma in my name Anthony Houston. Thompson didn't know where I was and I'm sure he didn't even know I was alive. He found me because Lashay recognized me from the church we both attend. If I was ever in a will I didn't know about it. I didn't even know he was the sperm that impregnated my mother until I was close to 19, by then I was plotting my way out. I didn't try to contact him then and I never have."

She pressed. Her motive clear, make Anthony, or anyone else the bad guy. Thompson was the true victim here. "Mr. Houston, are you or are you not aware that Pastor Thompson is a wealthy man?"

"I am aware that over the years he has taken in a substantial amount of money from real estate transactions and religious conferences."

"And isn't it true Mr. Houston, that you and the Pastor have had conversations about his wealth being transferred to you upon his death."

"Not in recent years."

"That'll be all." Somehow, she must have realized that the line of questioning was not approached properly. Her abrupt disruption of Anthony's response made that clear,

as did the way Thompson discreetly but apparently painfully squeezed her hand when she sat down. I assumed
it was painful because she delicately covered part of her
face with her free hand as though she was covering the
grimace.

Jason Ne, the lawyer Anthony hired to represent his
interests in the case did not miss her misstep. He continued the drive down the follow the money road.

"Mr. Houston, you indicate you all had not discussed
his wealth transferring to you in recent years. But there
was a discussion at some point?"

"Yes, there was."

"When was that discussion and what was the nature
of it?

"I think I was about 15, somewhere in that area. We
were on a crusade tour and he took me fishing in between
events. Aw man, now that I'm thinking about it, it was the
craziest conversation. One minute he's talking about not
really wanting to catch anything that day since we weren't
home and the next thing you know we're talking about
women."

Thompson's laugh shook the attention from the witness stand and clearly rattled a couple of the jurors. My
eyes caught the female attorney. She fidgeted in her seat.
His laugh, his presence crushed her. She seemed to fold
into the faux leather and wood chair. The judge's warning
look softened the volume of the laugh but did not stop
it. Anthony's face contorted like it was encountering the
worst stenches.

"You remember that day, don't you?"

Gavel in hand, the judge ordered the jury and court reporter to strike the last statements, admonishing him to only address the court.

"He asked if I knew what a woman's purpose was. I didn't answer. I didn't want to say the wrong thing and I didn't want him to know that I wasn't sure. He said women were originally created to share in what God was doing in the earth. But she was weak and manipulative, so her purpose was to give the only asset she has – her body. He told me that there are some women who believe they are valuable and women like that disrupt divine order."

The lady attorney jumped from her chair. "Your honor what does have to do with the matter at hand?"

Her objection overruled. She slowly sat down and once again Thompson's large, smooth hand blanketed hers.

"He told me that women are not to be trusted. You will use them for pleasure. You will trust them with nothing. You will be lord and man over every woman in every situation you deal with. He asked if I understood. I said I did. Then I asked why he was telling me those things. He said when he died, what he had would come to me and he wanted to make goddamned sure I didn't give his hard-earned money to a piece of ass. That's just how he laid it out there. Funny, now that you think about it – the thing he can't get enough of is what he was warning me about."

Thompson's laugh jolted us again, but what disturbed us was what he yelled. "And it's the thing you let make you soft."

Ne brought the attention back to the line of questioning. "Did he indicate how much money you might be entitled to?"

"No. I do know that none of the property or land believed to be the church's is in the name of the institution or corporation. Every piece of land, every building, and probably every bank account, at one point was in the name of some kind of trust and he was the sole trustee."

"So, again, just to be clear, as of this moment, in this courtroom do you have any knowledge of being an heir to anything owned by this man?" His basketball player length arms extended towards Thompson.

"No."

"Do you stand to gain anything personally from this trial or his conviction?"

"Yes."

"And what would that be?"

"For lack of a better word or understanding – closure."

I will never forget the day Thompson was convicted. Picture this - he stands and adjusts his tie. He unbuttons his coat and smooths his shirt, places his designer wire frames on his face and looks at the cameras set up near the rear of the room. The court police are cuffing him, he smiles, his eyes seductive in their glare; he is full control of the situation as he delivers a sermon.

Second Timothy three and 12 says, "Yea, and all that will live godly in Christ Jesus shall suffer persecution. Just as Jesus was betrayed, my sheep have betrayed me here today. Yet, I remain steadfast and unmovable. For your misjudgment of me, I am promised in verses eight and nine of that same book, Now, as Jannes and Jambres withstood Moses, so do these also resist the truth: men of corrupt minds, reprobate concerning the faith. But they shall proceed no further: for their folly shall be manifest unto all *men*, as theirs also was."

Two towers stood feet away from each other; though the energy that filled the space made it feel like inches. Thompson resolute and determined that there was nothing this court had done that would or could confine him. Anthony even more resolved and more determined. In that moment, you could literally feel the heat from their bodies filling the environment. The atmosphere became so heavy, that it seemed coughing was all I could do. It wasn't just me, something was happening and it did not feel good. Someone yelled the most sorrowful wail I'd ever heard; and the judge banged his gavel. If he said anything, I didn't hear it. The courtroom was suspended in some supernatural realm – it seemed – and as crazy as it sounds, until Thompson or Anthony released us, we would be held hostage.

"Michael guards the throne and deity of God like no other. Surely, you believe that is what you have done here. Surely, you have not. Just as the prison shook and released Paul, the same will happen for me. But I applaud you – son – you came for me with boldness." Thompson's smile and upright broad shoulders never shifted. You could see and feel why thousands had fallen prey to him. My God, in all honesty, the man was beautiful and he was a master of intellectual and spiritual chess. The officers attempts to remove him from his stage was again momentarily halted.

"Surely, you believe your own foolishness. Here is what I am certain of, First Peter three, somewhere around verse 13, "And who is there to harm you if you prove zealous for what is good? But even if you should suffer for the sake of righteousness, you are blessed. And do not fear their intimidation, and do not be troubled, but sanctify Christ as Lord in your hearts, always being ready to make a defense to everyone who asks you to give an account for the hope that is in you, yet with gentleness and reverence; and keep a good conscience so that in the thing in which you are slandered, those who revile your good behavior in Christ may be put to shame. For it is better, if God should will it so, that you suffer for doing what is right rather than for doing what is wrong." Anthony's word released the room. The blanket of uncertainty that had draped us in those seconds was gone. The wailing and the yells sprang from every angle of the space.

The judge's gavel pounded on the bench. "Enough, take him out of here. Mr. Houston sit down! Order and quiet in this court." He turned to his judicial assistant, and with more concern than I was comfortable seeing ordered her to get additional security personnel in the courtroom. His order was followed by another. Thompson's final remarks in the case. He yelled them across his shoulders, his smile gone and his face stern like a parent scolding a child.

"But evil men and seducers shall wax worse and worse, deceiving, and being deceived. But continue thou in the things which thou hast learned and hast been assured of, knowing of whom thou hast learned *them.*"

Four men in dark suits, and those black loafers sprang from their seats and exited the courtroom quickly. Seconds later a small army of deputies and bailiffs filed into the courtroom and began escorting emotionally spent women and men out of the courtroom. Order, at least in the courtroom restored, the judge dismissed the jury and directed deputies to escort each to their vehicles.

Stepping into the hallway outside of Courtroom 320B, I stepped into a media frenzy. This case fascinated them. Not since Yahweh Ben Yahweh had South Florida witnessed something like this. Federal charges, according to the reporters, were being considered as were charges in Akron and Trenton. I felt a stare engulfing me and followed its pull. Anthony slowly walked towards me. I wanted to run. I wanted to hear what he wanted to say. I wanted to know why he had never bothered to tell me the things I'd heard. I wanted to know if he knew I felt like every year I'd spent in his arms seemed like a horrible fairy tale. When his arms moved to pull me in, I suddenly found my body, and my strength and – ran.

*That name means
something to me*

Chapter Fifteen

Anthony gave me room for quite a while after his confrontation with Thompson and the trial. On the stand and often in tears he also told his mother's story, his sister's story, Nisa's story, Lashira's story and finally his. Anthony had never been physically chastised, he had never been victimized like the others; instead he was being trained and groomed to administer the varying assaults that molded the church. He was the first-born son and therefore heir to Thompson's throne. It was a position he never sought; primarily because he didn't know it was his to be had. After knowing Christ for himself, he also knew that it was a demonic position and not one that God had called him to.

Several days after the jury's decision and watching officers lead wounded lives away, I came home to find Ant there. When I stepped into our bedroom my heart filled with so many emotions I could not distinguish one from the other. I knew that I didn't like the sight of him packing. Yet, I could not stop him.

"Hey, where have you been?"

"At Nisa's. I've been keeping my cell on and charged just in case." He slowly laid his dress shirts across the bed.

"May I ask you something baby?"

"If I said no, would that stop you?"

I smiled. "Probably not. Where did Anthony Houston come from?"

"I'm not sure I understand your question."

"The name and the man; where did Anthony Houston come from?"

He motioned for me to join him in the chair that looked out into the garden. While I hesitated, I sat on his lap and waited for his explanation. I was still so mad and so hurt.

"The name is easy. Houston was a private detective. It was one of the first TV shows I saw outside of First Alliance when I traveled with Fujana. Anthony was the name of my best friend when I was a little boy. He died when he was seven, caught a cold one winter and never got better. But we were thick as thieves; there wasn't a day we weren't together until the moment he went home to glory. Anthony Houston. That name means something to me. Friendship and something from my first inkling of life outside. That's what I tried to tell you that day. I don't know Michael Thompson, Anthony never called me Michael and neither did my mother. She called me Bird and so did he. In the church, those who did not have a 'new' name, where often just referred to as son, or brother. As I got a little older they would call me Brother Preacher, because it was widely believed that there was a calling on my life to preach. Anthony Houston then came from a small group of people who fought in secret, died in turmoil but loved with everything in them. He came from a liberty granted in different ways by God."

He lifted me from his lap and rose to finish packing.

"It, ahm, was a long day in court. I guess having to testify in the other trials is overwhelming." He simply raised in eyebrows, acknowledging he heard my words. "You hungry?"

"You don't have to go out of your way. I was trying to be gone before you got here."

"It's no big thing. I've got to eat too. Besides I know Nisa can't cook."

"That she can't do. And let me tell you, it's hard getting used to Wendy's, Bojangles and McDonalds for every meal. Have you ever eaten a warmed-over chicken biscuit for breakfast?"

"That's not healthy baby. You have to eat right."

"Baby. Second time you called me that this evening. Is that because I've still got a chance or because you can't call me Anthony?"

"It's just the name that came to mind. Chicken or pork chops?"

"You..."

"Unh unh, nothing deep. Chicken or pork chops?"

"Your choice."

As I sliced potatoes for the salad and scrambled the onions and bell peppers for the green beans, I recounted the testimonies yet again. Anthony said on the stand that it was ironic that while Thompson did not destroy him inside the church, he had found a way to do it outside of the church. He had invaded his new life and managed to again tear love away from him. It finally hit me – Thompson's whole purpose in finding Anthony was to destroy his marriage. There was no other way he could get him. He had blamed Anthony for Lashira's inability to love him and therefore waited for Anthony to love again so that he could hopefully make me unable to love my husband. Truth of the matter is while I initially did not trust him after that day in the hotel, I never stopped loving him. I truly love him and hearing him say everything on the stand that I had not allowed him to say to me in the aftermath, helped me to understand that no man or woman would have an easy time of revealing everything that Anthony knew and had been through. The rational me got that. The romantic, insecure and scared me could not understand it and sadly that side of me was winning the battle.

I watched him sit his bags down at the front door with some remorse. I didn't know what to say or do in this situation. Maggie phoned to check on me earlier that day, and managed – in her uniquely nosy way – to ask if Anthony was back at home. When I said, no she asked "why not." With bitterness in my voice I retorted, "I'm not ready."

"You're not ready for what - to continue to love a man that will move heaven and earth to make sure you're happy. Let me tell your stubborn and selfish behind something, don't lose that kind of love because you think he should have told you something. Girl, I'm your best friend, have been since we were six and there are some things I don't tell you and have not told you."

"Maggie..."

"No, no. Listen to me. Girl sometimes you get involved in foolishness and it's the kind of stuff that you can't even explain to yourself let alone somebody else. You just package it up and put it in your closet and pray that those skeletons don't come tumbling out. Anthony didn't have a choice in what he was involved in, but he did make a choice to get out and that should say something."

"He didn't trust me Maggie."

"And apparently rightfully so. He knew he had been involved in some awful mess girl. Awful mess tearing down God's kingdom. And to know at the head of all of that is the man that fathered you. I wouldn't have told you, especially if I knew you'd walk away from me and that's what you did. Where's your compassion for your husband?"

I hung up on her. No one wants to hear the truth; especially when you've decided that you just want to be mad – real mad.

"Crys, I asked if you wanted me to take the garbage out before I go? Listen, if you're not comfortable with this - I can just grab something on the way back to Nisa's."

"No, no. It's fine. Dinner's ready. I was thinking about something Maggie said to me today. That's all."

"She's been checking on me. She's even been praying with me."

"Maggie's been praying with you? That's funny."

"I know right. I think she's doing it, because she knows you're not."

"That's not fair boy."

"You're right. I miss you and even though I'm sure it won't be received right now; I still love you like I have never loved anyone else in my life. For the record that includes LaShira."

I nearly stumbled at the mention of her name. I had been pondering where I stacked up in his heart against her. Rather than dig up that bone, I took the comment for what it was and carefully laid the plate over-laden with dinner before him and turned to the frig for the iced tea. This felt so strange, this whole having dinner with my husband. He looked the same except he seemed to have lost a good 30 pounds, but he didn't feel the same. He spoke the same, but the wisdom of the weeks slowed his pace. He moved the same, but the weight of the past and the present had taken some of this thickness. He was a familiar stranger. I poured the tea and set the pitcher before him. I could smell the coconut oil permeating from his scalp and without any thought kissed him softly in the center of his dome. He took a deep breath and smiled. About half an hour later, when he had dried the dishes and taken out the trash, he grabbed his bags and left. For the first time since the day I left the hotel parking lot that day, I cried. This time I cried for my husband.

In the month, three weeks and two days that we were apart after dinner that night - God took the time to remind me that there was a purpose for Anthony and me to find each other, and I couldn't allow my doubting nature to tear apart what He had put together. God had to point out that it was Anthony's past that brought him closer to Him and that unconditional love, meant forgiving someone's past just the way He forgives ours. God reminded me that despite how horrific Anthony's past was it had led to tremendous faith and miraculous super-natural deliverance. God, the wonderful marriage counselor that He is, also told me to check myself. Not only did

I not listen to or wait on my husband, I didn't even wait on Him.

Having been thoroughly chastised and re-assured; and after putting the final touches on Anthony's story for Upscale Magazine, I called my baby's cell late one night and said come home. Forty-five seconds later I heard a sound I had missed so much – his key turning in the door.

"You told me to come home. What's that confused look all about?" He seemed to hesitate moving towards me.

"Nisa's place is a good 15-minute drive, with no traffic."

"I ... truth .... I've been staying with Nisa, but every night I sleep right out there in my car, sometimes in the gazebo. I needed to know you were okay."

"Even though I didn't want to love you?"

"Because until you told me otherwise, I still have a role in your life and part of that role is to protect you. Crys, are you sure about this? Can I come home – completely?"

When he stepped into the foyer, this time the emotions were certain. I love this man. I am happy to see this man. This man is still mine and I have been a fool to even think about never calling him back home. Even though he looked like he needed a shave and a good night's sleep, I enjoyed the sight of him. I enjoyed the smell of the coconut oil and the car air freshener on his t-shirt. I enjoyed the rough feel of his jeans when he picked me up and held me against his waist.

"Baby girl I've been waiti...."

"It's all right Anthony. I love you and I trust you. I'm sorry I let ..."

"Don't be. There's so much waiting for us now that the demons are gone. And I'm sorry baby. I am so sorry."

We held each other for hours that night. I kept touching him all over like I had to be sure he was all there and nothing was missing. He just smiled. Every once in a while, he'd kiss my fingers and put my hand against his heart. It was beating. That is good. Then I would start my inspection all over again. I think we were both afraid to make love although all the signs physically and emotionally were there. I think we were both also a little afraid to fall asleep. Finally, after I heard Anthony thank God for restoration, I nestled my back against his side and we both fell into deep slumber. In the chill of the night, I reached for the blanket but found Anthony instead. When I did, the act of making love became so easy and so powerful until I literally felt like we were pouring our all into each other to assure no spot was left unloved. We made love hard and long enough to regain every tender moment we had lost. He slowed his pace at one point long enough to kiss the tears on my cheek and so I returned the favor.

*Your real deliverance is
tied up*

Chapter Sixteen

Warren told me he was glad he made the decision to leave me at the hotel that day. Not only because Anthony and I needed to get to that moment of full disclosure, but because of what he witnessed. The girl they threw into the van was taken to an old farm style house on Card Sound Road, where she was to be prepared to nourish the pastor and one of his sons. When the young woman protested, a group of eight women beat her into submission and then bathed her in soothing salts so that the wounds would quickly heal. She was admonished for being unwilling to present her body as a living sacrifice. Warren and a team of officers arrested eighteen people at the home that day and took six girls, none over 15 into protective custody. Two of the six said Thompson was their natural father.

Warren while being nosy as people were arrested, learned from a deacon that Thompson had a mission, set Anthony up or destroy what we had – either way he would imprison him. Either in a state facility or in a mental or emotional prison from whence he would not recover; that confirmed what God had revealed. Thompson had planned to do the same thing to me he'd done to Nisa, hang me on a cross and rape me to his satisfaction. The key difference however was that he had apparently decided to kill me and leave me in my husband's bed dressed in Lashira's choir robe. What manner of evil is this?

Cathy English was arrested for aiding in the false imprisonment of Nisa and I. She confirmed the rape and murder plot that Warren uncovered. The judge gave her probation and ordered psychiatric treatment because three court ordered doctors questioned her mental capacity. I saw her at church one day and she again talked to me about getting her little sister. I did find out, during the trial, that the little sister was really her daughter. The rest of her story was probably someone else's. Glenice was in protective custody. Anthony recognized Cathy because he knew Glenice and they looked alike. His mother took her for a walk in the woods one night into Anthony's arms and told him to find a home for the little bird. She was five. Glenice was clear on one thing - she never wanted to see any of them ever again. Even at five, she had seen several beatings and had never learned to sleep through the night. When Cathy approached me yet again about the matter, I pinned her against the wall and encouraged her to "get counseling, your real deliverance is tied up in the confusion in your head, and by the way your child is fine and does not wish to see you." Would you believe that Cathy is only 27, Glenice just turned 14?

While God had granted me divine understanding of the whole ordeal, Anthony and I, in the whole beginning-to-heal process, had a thorough and long conversation about his former involvement with First Born and what came out of him that day in the hotel room. Watching the tears fall from his eyes in front of me, I had a new level of understanding about his need for and the depth of his relationship with God. He took it so seriously, didn't allow anyone to discount it and there was nothing in life now that he didn't consult with God about. Most of what we talked about that day I had already heard on the stand, but it was re-assuring to hear him say those things to me personally. It was good for him to cry it out in a way he couldn't do on the stand and it was right that I held him as he worked through it.

Together we decided that the acceptance of carnality and the extreme pressure to serve the pastor or be chastised for it; had become too normal a practice at Rev. Brighton's church. We also admitted to each other that I and we probably should have left just based on Brighton's sexual advances toward me. Even more troubling was that the whole air at Triumph had become too close to home in many respects to what had happened in First Born. Trusting that God would lead us to the right house to worship, we left. For several weeks, we visited different churches. Sometimes, we would worship at home under my husband's teaching. It was something so unbelievably erotic about him teaching. One day as he read from the Song of Solomon, I remembered thinking, "God, can I keep him?"

The house of worship we finally ended up in was Bethel Community Church. Anthony submitted his license for consideration and began working as an Associate Minister. Soon after that when the pastor retired, they offered Anthony a pastoral contract and he accepted. For the first six months, he focused on redirecting hearts, minds, talents, and treasures to God – not the pastor and not the church. He seemed to have to fight to get people to understand that serving God and the kingdom had more meaning than just assuring that the pastor knew you were involved in 12 things. That effective ministry is holistic; you must first serve your family and yourself and assure that you are healthy in every regard so that the Lord can use you based on His will. Loyalty, he taught is not in how diligent you are in the church but how diligent you are in your Christ and in your relationship with Him. If you are in church eight nights a week, he taught, yet you've not heard from God - that's because you're too loyal to the church and not loyal enough to the Lord. Amazingly, after the initial shock of the teachings, the church is beginning to grow. Healthy and balanced families come out of a healthy and balanced church, that's what Anthony believes and therefore that's what Bethel is taught to believe and practice.

The man I would stare at and think 'finally' was back. We found each other all over again on an even more intense level. We found each other on a level that the angels must have with God; where just his presence fills me with something I cannot explain. That something often leaves me with tears clinging to my eyelids. This new love in Anthony was like experiencing glory during pain. It felt better than anything I could ever have imagined, especially after that day in the hotel stairway when I told my husband, that he was a stranger to me and one I never wanted to see again.

Warren, in uncovering everything that was building in the house on Card Sound Road found a journal that belonged to Anthony's birth mother. We would spend evenings reading it, healing his pain and getting to know the woman who fought to leave so that her children could live. In one note she said she thought to name him Sorrow, because of what he would be born into and what he was conceived in. Instead God told her he had a calling on his unborn life and that his pain would make way for Kingdom blessings. Still the hell that she lived in was more than her heart could handle and the hell outweighed her trust in God and that's why she decided to take her life. The last letter she wrote; she addressed directly to her unborn son – Jeshua Elijah.

In the discovery, were also some personal effects of Ant's mom and sister. Each time he pulled out something new, he'd come running to me like a little boy with his first kindergarten drawing. There was a picture of his mom and Darmisha. Miss Lucille, the woman that raised him was right, even as a little thing Darmisha was every bit of her mother. She had large dark eyes that seemed to jump out of her head. They both had beautiful long, dark hair. Anthony would cry. He missed his sister and now he missed his mother. Then the next day, it would be the same thing over again. He'd find a piece of jewelry or a letter. Darmisha wrote poetry and he would often find poems, some she had not completed. I started pulling it all together, the poetry and the letters for a book. They deserved that I thought, it was my way of connecting with the part of our family I'd been robbed of.

I now know that this is my family too and because it is where Anthony came from, it is where I came from. Nisa was excited about the book project and Ant and I discovered that she has a very natural gift for writing. I mean the girl is fierce and I told her, her mom would be proud of her talent. It was Nisa that completed the poems her mom did not. Thompson had failed. We were a family after all. It was the manifestation of what Anthony's mom had written in a letter, "there is a beautiful joy in knowing the destruction someone has written over your life, can be erased with a simple stroke from the Son." It is a beautiful joy indeed.

Anthony drug in from what appeared to be a long energy-diminishing day. Yet, his smile grew curious as he walked into the kitchen and found me cooking. He sauntered up behind me kissing me, cupping my breasts and massaging my nipples after tugging on the hem of my shirt beneath my apron.

"Nisa's here tonight."

"Ah man. Where is she?"

"Out in the gazebo, doing some editing for me."

"Okay, well..."

"No boy! Set the table."

"Yes ma'am. How was your day?"

"Cool. Me and Nisa hung out, went to the mall did some shopping, she got her navel pierced."

"She did what?"

I pulled him into my arms as he attempted to get out the back door to the garden. "Nisa is a grown woman. You need to start looking at her that way. She's got a man and all."

"She's gotta what?"

"A man. A romantic interest. A boo. She's in love and she'd tell you if you stopped thinking she's still a little girl."

"I know. I just .... I know you're right. She is very pretty and very smart. She's so much like her mom - energy and fire, quiet and creative. She's all right now, isn't she?"

"She's as all right as you are. And that's a good thing."

We watched her from the kitchen window together, holding each other. I turned to pull the meatloaf out of the oven when the timer sang. I felt Anthony's eyes watching me.

"What are you doing enjoying the fragrance like you did that night I met you?"

"Aah, what a nice fragrance it was and still is too." He ducked to avoid the flying dish towel. "I was actually wondering how far along you are."

"What did you say?"

"I said, I was wondering how far along you are."

"How did you....? You make me oh so sick. Couldn't I have just told you this weekend in the Bahamas like I'd planned. How'd you know?"

"Girl I know the feel of your body better than you do. I know where every freckle is, where every mark is and I know if they move a quarter inch. I know, Lord have mercy, how your breasts rest in my hands and they've been resting a bit differently. LORD HAVE MERCY! And I know how often I'm going to get sent to the drug store because you ran out of pads again. I haven't been in a minute."

He was right. Not only was the Bethel family experiencing growth, but so is our family. It turns out the fainting spells, nausea and other little symptoms were not just the evil of Thompson in our lives, but they were also symptomatic of my pregnancy. Jeshua Elijah Houston is due in six months, on the day of his grandmother's birth. Now I understand his parents had to and must fight the evil that doesn't want him here – nor did it want him conceived. But I sleep securely knowing that his deliverance into purpose and destiny is sheltered in mighty prayer and a relationship of faith that will endure.

Bound for Hell

Chapter
Seventeen

The phone ringing woke me from a very nice and needed nap. Jeshua is all boy and every bit of his father. Even at three months old, he must be doing something, reaching for something, pulling on something, laughing about something. He is quite an active little bundle. A bundle I love immensely. I reached over to pull the receiver from the cradle and check the caller ID. It was a number I didn't recognize.

I called it back thinking maybe it was Anthony calling from a client's office. It was anything but that. I had unknowingly called a corrections facility in West Miami Dade. The security officer said a young lady there was very distraught after visiting an inmate before he was shipped out and asked if I would come pick her up. She handed the receiver to the woman.

"Hello, who is this?" I couldn't understand her through the tears. "Who is this?"

"It's me Auntie Crys. It's Nisa. I just..."

"Nisa, why are you there? Why are you there?" My screaming woke Jeshua, whose crying notified me that was not a good thing. I scooped him up from the bed, pulling him to my bosom and cradled the phone between my head and my shoulder. Running through the house, I hoped Anthony was home after all. "Talk to me sweetie. Why are you there?"

"I came to see him, because I found a note he wrote to grandma telling her she could leave, God no longer needed or wanted her. I got mad and I wanted to ...."

As she talked, I yelled for Ant when I saw his car in the drive-way. Finally, he came running through the garden door off the kitchen. He took Jeshua from my arms thinking something was wrong with him. I pointed to the phone and tried to tell him what was going on.

"Nisa, went to see Thompson..." He snatched the phone.

"Nisa what were you thinking? What happened? What happened?"

The security officer took the phone and explained what Nisa could not. "The inmate, we assume thought he was out of camera view. The young lady sat down in the holding cell and was talking with him. Apparently, he took advantage of a guard being out of eye range. He moved the chair close to her, blocking her against the wall. He fondled her breast and he stroked her vaginal area through her jeans before the guard rushed in and stopped him." The officer said he would face additional charges, if the victim pressed them.

When Anthony brought Nisa home that night she was still shaking like a leaf. No one said anything. I rocked her. Anthony sat on the floor, playing and tussling with Jeshua. Jeshua giggled. He loves playing with his father. While he's a thick baby, sometimes I think Ant's a bit rough with him. The ringing phone startled all of us, Anthony answered it, and said a few indistinguishable things. Placing it back on the cradle, he settled back on the floor with his son. After several moments of silence, tears slowly trickled down his chiseled cheeks. He turned to face Nisa and I; Jeshua's little face resting against his chest.

"Thompson had a heart attack on the way to Avon Park. He's bound for hell - finally."

Nisa hugged him and reached for me to join them on the floor. Was it relief in the air or was it hoping this was the finalization of his evil? Whatever it was, Nisa prayed for her grandmother, her mother, her uncle, her stepfather and "every angel that lost their wings in the hell fire that was First Alliance." Then she prayed that she and those who still live could forgive him, so that their deliverance was not held hostage in hell.

 **E. Claudette Freeman** spent some 24 years in radio in South Florida, before leaving to obtain her Certified Life Coaching Credentials through the American Association of Christian Therapists and to start her own media corporation, Emily C. Freeman Holdings, LLC. The company does business through E. Claudette Freeman Literary Services which provides an array of writing services including: coaching, editing, commissioned stage/film works and publishing consulting. Employing literary principles and styling to empowerment modules, Freeman also hosts Arise Through Your Spirit, in home/conference and workplace based life coaching programs.

www.ingramcontent.com/pod-product-compliance
Lightning Source LLC
Chambersburg PA
CBHW071314250626
47159CB00004B/1414